INTO RUIN

HOCKEY TITANS

S. MASSERY

To those who crave darkness

INTRODUCTION

Hello dear reader!

If you've read me before (especially my Hockey Gods series), you know they run quite dark.

This book contains themes common to dark romance, including bullying, blackmail, stalking, non consent and dubious consent, and somnophilia. Also, perhaps, a little murder.

Camden Church asked me to remind you that some secrets are better left in the dark.

xoxo,
Sara

A QUICK NOTE IF YOU READ TAKE ME TO CHURCH

The short story titled *Take Me to Church* originally appeared in the Bookish Box Anthology Volume II.

The storyline in TMtC was nixed, and a lot of minor and major details were changed. Because of this, it is considered an 'alternate universe'. The version of Camden Church in that story does not exist anymore. The heroine was changed entirely.

This does not affect the Church you met in Hockey Gods.

I'm sorry for the confusion, and I hope you enjoy the new and improved *Into Ruin* version of college-aged Camden Church.

xo, Sara

Music thrums through the hockey house. It's so loud it vibrates in my chest. I grip the strap of my bag tighter and make my way deeper inside, searching for one familiar face.

The *only* familiar face.

There are a million people packed inside, and I squeeze through narrow gaps. No one really looks at me. I'm the perennial wallflower everywhere I go. It hasn't really mattered before, though. I don't *want* people looking at me.

Finally, I catch a glimpse of Royal. He's standing with a group of guys, plus one bottle-blond, model-thin girl. Her hair is curled, and her jean shorts are cropped so much her ass cheeks are hanging out. Paired with glittery cowboy boots and a flannel shirt she has knotted above her navel...

I'm not surprised most of Royal's friends stare at her instead of focusing on him.

He, however, seems bored. His gaze coasts around,

only pausing when it lands on me. His eyes light up, and he waves me over.

I swallow sharply, but as soon as I'm within arm's reach, he reels me in. His arm drops around my shoulders, locking me to his side.

"Guys, Marcy, this is my baby sister, Harper." He jostles me a little. "She's a freshman."

I incline my chin.

"New meat," one of the guys says, holding out his fist to be bumped by one of the others. "Nice."

Royal glares at him. "Abso-fucking-lutely not."

I shift my weight. Accepting Royal's invite... not my first choice.

"Thought you had changed your mind," he says in a low voice. "You seem...?"

"I walked in on my roommate and her boyfriend screwing on her desk." I shudder. "I need alcohol to get this out of my brain."

Royal nods sagely. "You've come to the right place. I just have one rule."

I raise my eyebrow. He said nothing about *rules*. He's a sophomore. He pretends to know better than me, but he's barely more than a year older. Definitely not wiser.

"No fucking my teammates." He nudges me and points toward the kitchen. "Drinks in there. My room is first on the left upstairs, you can stash your bag there."

Right.

I leave the safety of his side and venture into the kitchen. A full bar has been set up on the counters, red cups stacked next to the alcohol. On the porch outside is a big, metal keg. I wrinkle my nose and go toward one of the bottles of clear liquor. I'm not picky… I have no experience.

I pull one out at random and scan the label.

Vodka.

I splash it into a cup and add orange juice, give it a little finger-stir, and exit the kitchen with my index finger in my mouth just as a new wave of people enter. I sip the drink and wince at the burn. But that's the point, right? Alcohol isn't supposed to be *fun* to drink.

Someone bumps into me, sending my bag flying off my shoulder. It's zipped shut, but I dive for it anyway. My face flames. I clutch my bag under my arm, my drink firmly clenched in my other fist, and head toward the staircase.

No one calls out to me. I'm certainly not dressed for a party—my hoodie and jeans aren't really the aesthetic of most of the girls here—and I'm not going to pretend either. I slip through under the radar and finally get some breathing room on the stairs. I dodge around couples making out and pause at the rope across the top of the stairs.

DO NOT ENTER, the sign hanging from it says.

I step over it.

First door on the right is his, he said? I go to it and push the door open, expecting an empty room. After all, there was a sign. *A rope.*

But nope.

There's a girl on the desk, her legs open wide, and a guy between them. It takes a minute to realize it's not my brother—*thank fucking God*—but then… I don't know. I keep watching. Maybe I'm curious? Horrified?

Both at the same time?

This is the second fucking couple I've walked in on. I'm cursed. I must be. I mean—can't a girl catch a break?

Deciding to follow Royal was one thing.

This...

This is just not cool.

The guy is fucking the girl like he hates her. I only saw a glimpse of my roommate and her boyfriend, but they weren't going at it like this. The whole desk moves with every thrust. His bare ass is pointed right at me, muscles tensing and straining. His head is bowed, his gaze locked on her bare chest.

"We've got an audience," the girl moans.

The guy slows and glances over his shoulder.

Definitely not my brother. His gaze rakes up and down my body, and I automatically tighten the grip on the strap of my bag. And my cup.

Do I play it cool?

Do I run away?

"Just a little voyeur," the guy finally says. "I don't mind, do you?"

I swallow hard.

The girl seems to crash back down to earth at that. Her glare spears me. "Get out, bitch."

That just... rubs me the wrong way. I take a long sip of the drink and stay where I am. It's a choice now, instead of being locked into place by fear or surprise. I backed down with my roommate—I fled like I was the one in trouble.

She didn't even *warn* me. No sock on the doorknob,

no text. No TEXT! We're in the twenty-first century and I got *nothing*.

Whatever.

I'm not bitter. She wasn't doing it on my bed, at any rate.

Royal's desk, however...

I wrinkle my nose.

"Stop her, baby."

Also gross.

The guy sighs. He steps away and roughly drags his jeans back into place, and the girl freezes. Legs spread. It's dark, so I'm spared the details, but she seems to be glitching in place.

"What are you doing?"

He shakes his head and motions for the door. "Your whining is making my cock soft. You should go."

"But—"

"Out." Jeans secure, he crosses his arms over his chest. He's still wearing a shirt, *and* he kept his pants on, which means he stripped her—or she stripped herself—and he didn't reciprocate.

She slides off the desk and hunts for her clothes. Panties, dress. No bra, not that she retrieves anyway. She fluffs her hair, her scowl aimed first at him and then me. She snatches her phone off the edge of the desk.

When she passes me, she knocks her shoulder into mine.

I barely manage to keep from spilling the drink all over me.

And now...

"Little voyeur," the guy says. "Was it jealousy that made you stay? Or is that truly your kink?"

"It's definitely not." I shake my head. "I was looking for Royal's room. You're—"

"His is across the hall." He saunters forward.

I tense, but I'm not going to be run off. There's a challenge in his gaze. His eyes are deep blue, his hair dark and unruly. He steps up close to me and flicks the switch by my elbow. A lamp in the corner comes on behind him.

"Royal won't fuck you," he continues. "He's got a pretty hot girlfriend who would cut his balls off if he did."

My jaw drops.

"Not saying you're not hot," he adds. "You've got that girl-next-door vibe. The sweatshirt and jeans, your messy bun hair..."

He grabs my bag's strap and tugs it off my shoulder. I reach for it, but he moves away too fast.

And I make the mistake of entering his room fully.

"What's your name?" He cocks his head.

I frown and follow him. He sidesteps me, and before I know it, he closes the door and leans against it. My bag dangles from his fingertips.

"Name," he repeats, his tone hardening.

"Harper."

"Well, *Harper*, you cost me tonight."

I roll my eyes. "I cost you a cheap lay, it seemed like. You didn't even take your pants all the way off."

He lets my bag fall from his hand, and his fingers land on the doorknob. With a slight twist, he locks it.

For the first time, a sliver of awareness slides through me. He's cute—no, no, he's devastatingly handsome—but that doesn't mean he's safe. It's never quite translated that way in my limited experience.

I take a step back, and he smirks.

"I should go."

He doesn't move. His gaze sharpens, watching me

carefully. When I swallow, his attention falls to my throat. Then lower. I'm grateful for the oversized hoodie, the thick fabric that doesn't cling to my curves. Even though, right now, it feels like I'm more exposed than the girl who was just spread naked on his desk.

"You have to pay the toll to pass," he says.

"You could go out there and easily find another girl to fuck." I shake my head. "Instead, you're trying to talk me into it?"

"I don't want to fuck you."

I still. A mixture of relief and uncertainty course through me. If not sex—

"I'd settle for a blow job."

"No." I stare at him. "Absolutely not."

"Don't worry, little voyeur. The door is locked. No one will walk in on us. Our little secret." He tilts his head again, appraising me. "Unless you're an exhibitionist, too."

"I'm not either." I grit my teeth and glance around the room. "And it's in poor taste to borrow a room during a party just to have sex with some girl on a desk."

He laughs. "Yeah. Like it's in *poor taste* to throw yourself at a hockey player."

"I wasn't."

"Of course not."

I stare at him.

"I can give you another option," he eventually replies.

"Great." I raise my hand in a *come on* motion. "Let's hear that."

"You give me your bra and panties."

I wrinkle my nose. "What the fuck for?"

He lifts a shoulder. "Tax. Toll. Fucking penance. Take your pick."

My face flames as I consider it. I go to the window and look out at the backyard. There are more people out back than there were in the front. A fire in a pit crackles, sending embers floating into the sky. Groups of people are gathered out there. The pulse of music, while fainter here, can still be felt.

There's nothing on this side of the house to help me down. Going out the window is... not happening.

Blow job or giving up my underwear?

I shake my head carefully and unbutton my jeans.

The guy behind me lets out a low whistle.

My sweatshirt hides most of my ass when I wriggle the jeans down, then my panties. They're black with red hearts all over them. Cotton. Full coverage. *Not sexy in the slightest.* I have to take my shoes and jeans all the way off to untangle myself. The cool autumn wind brushes my bare legs.

I straighten, clutching the thin fabric. It's warm from being pressed to my body.

And he's right there.

In front of me.

He pushes me back against the window, and my ass hits the sill.

"W-what are you doing?"

"Changed my mind," he says roughly. "You gonna scream, Harper? Will you fight me?"

I—

I don't know.

I stare at him, and instantly, I'm turned on. Like a switch flipping, I go from scared to *intrigued*. I bite the inside of my cheek, fighting the rush of adrenaline.

He reaches around me and closes the window. I lean on the glass when his fingers go to the insides of my knees.

I don't know his name, and he's tracing a path up my inner thigh. To a spot no one's touched in a really fucking long time.

My eyes flutter shut when he gets to my pussy. He pushes a finger inside me, and I let out a low whimper. It just comes out, escaping past my teeth.

This is really fucking wrong.

He slides the single digit in and out, the friction cranking my arousal. It's not enough to get me over the edge, and I grip the windowsill to keep still. It builds, slowly. I can't look at him. My eyes are screwed shut.

The sensation disappears, and suddenly, I'm sliding off the sill.

To my knees.

I gasp, and his cock presses into my mouth. He doesn't wait—my eyes pop open, but he has me caught. His hand in my hair, his hips thrusting forward.

"Be a good girl," he orders.

My mouth opens wider, and he sneers. His lips hold a cruel tilt. His grip tightens, tugging at my bun, his nails scratching along my scalp.

This isn't a blow job.

When he moves, he *fucks*. I imagine it's a similar sight to the one I walked in on—but this time, it's my face accepting the brunt of it. He hits the back of my throat, then pushes deeper. I gag around him, my throat constricting, and he groans.

He pulls out, then back in. Deeper. I reach up, but he catches my hand in his, pinning it on top of the one already in my hair.

I take snatches of breath when I can. Saliva runs out of my mouth. Tears prick my eyes.

My other, traitorous hand finds its way between my legs. I touch myself to distract—but it just adds to the sensations. The pain in my scalp, the burn in my lungs.

Fuck.

How did this happen?

He groans and shudders and abruptly pulls out. He cranks my head back and releases my hand. He strokes himself once, twice, and then comes.

On my face.

I close my eyes tight as the hot ropes of cum hit my cheeks, my lips, my nose and chin.

His fingers slip from my hair, and he steps back. His presence looming over me disappears, and I sag back to sit on my heels. I carefully wipe at my eyes, then open them. He's already put back together. Jeans in place, shirt smoothed. I don't know if he ever took it off.

"Not bad," he says. "Usually, they try to take over. You just... let it happen."

I swallow my reply and climb to my feet. My knees knock together. It's like I just went on a roller coaster. The adrenaline has left me shaky. I brace myself on the window and watch him move back to the door. He crouches next to my bag, unzips it, and dips into it.

"Hey—" My voice cracks, hoarse from the beating he just bestowed on my throat.

"Shh." He finds my student ID in my wallet, which lists what dorm I'm in. He takes his phone from his pocket and snaps a picture of it. "Until next time, Harper Shay."

Then he unlocks the door and slips out.

3

CAMDEN

"Hey!" Royal knocks on my door. "You quit early."

The party has finally died out. I'm flat on my bed, but I haven't yet bothered to change out of my jeans. The lamp in the corner, that bathed Harper in shadows as I fucked her mouth, is still on. I left only long enough for her to put herself back together and get the hell out of my room, minus one thing.

Her panties are in my pocket.

They're burning a hole there, but I haven't yet taken them out. Haven't touched them since I slid them in there while touching her hot cunt. She was wet. Practically dripping. But I can't figure out why. Was it my threat? Getting in her space? Or lingering arousal from *watching*?

I meant what I said. She's hot in the girl-next-door way. She was clearly not there to party, which made it all the weirder that she came upstairs. Girls who try to seduce one of us usually put more effort in.

I'm pretty sure she was wearing a sports bra under

that hoodie. I didn't see it, but... well, I've seen enough breasts in push-up bras, or underwire, to know the difference.

"Earth to Church." Royal shakes his head, leaning on the doorjamb. "You okay?"

I sit up. "Just didn't feel like going through the whole charade tonight."

He nods slowly. "You still feel like you're on a pedestal?"

I grunt.

I'm the novelty. I've been the novelty.

Luckily, my teammates didn't see me that way. I had practiced with the team before I accepted a spot at Framingham State University. And when I was drafted second overall at the NHL draft this past June, it was with the franchise's knowledge and support I spend the next two years playing college hockey.

The media coverage went hard for a few weeks, but things have calmed down. I've learned to shut out *that* noise. It's just the school's noise that seems harder to ignore.

"My sister is gonna crash in my room tonight," he says.

I raise an eyebrow. "You have a sister?"

"Half sister. Our mom divorced my dad and married hers. And I don't talk about her much because I know how assholes can be. They hear *baby sister* and think *how fast can I get in her pants?* It's disgusting."

"Right..."

He shudders. "I swear, she can date whoever she

wants, just not one of my teammates. That asshole wouldn't make it out of FSU alive."

I snicker. "If she's hot, good luck."

"Don't."

I hold up my hands in surrender. "No, no, of course not. So where did this sister come from? Is she visiting or something?"

"She's a freshman. Her name is Harper, just in case you run into her in the morning or something." He glances out my window. "Although it's practically morning already."

My blood runs cold.

Harper?

Sister?

I cling on to a normal, even expression. "Yeah, I'm gonna get to sleep while I still can."

"Same. Night, Church."

He closes my door, and I immediately stand. I lock the door and open my phone, going to the photo of her student ID.

Freshman dorm.

Harper Shay.

She doesn't look like Royal Lawson. She doesn't have his last name. She—

If she tells him what I did, he could sabotage me. From the sounds of his threat, he *would* do whatever he could to get retribution. I wasn't gentle with her, not in the slightest. The truth could mean saying goodbye to my career—my future.

She let me think she was trying to hook up with him, and

that couldn't have been further from the truth. She didn't deny my accusations. It was her trump card. Royal's sister could've come out with it, and I would've stepped aside.

But she didn't.

My jaw tightens.

She's not going to get away with this.

4

___

HARPER

That's mainly the truth. Royal slept on the floor, leaving me the bed in his room, and I tossed and turned all night. I stole a pair of boxers from his dresser to wear, then didn't bother giving them back when I tugged my jeans on at eight o'clock this morning.

The door to the room across the hall was shut when I scurried out.

Now, I brush out my hair in my room, fresh out of a scalding-hot shower. I scrubbed my skin until it was red, washed my face a few times, and then just stood under the stream. No amount of bar soap in the guys' shared bathroom was enough to rid me of the sensation of cum on my face.

And the lingering humiliation.

Why did I let that happen?

Why didn't I just...

I exhale.

Someone knocks on the door, interrupting my train of thought. My roommate and her boyfriend were gone when I returned, but she wouldn't knock.

I glance down at myself. Everything is secure—my body, I mean—under a towel. My wet hair hangs over my shoulder.

The knock comes again. Harder.

I go and crack it—and freeze.

The guy from last night reaches out and shoves my door in, immediately filling the space and slipping inside.

"You—What are you doing?" I catch the door and hold it open. "Get out."

He stops in the middle of my room and turns in a small circle. Analyzing everything, from my roommate's messy side to my made bed. The rows of pictures attached to strings and lights on her wall. My relatively empty shelves, minus the textbooks I'll need this semester.

There's noise in the hallway, and I release the door automatically. It swings shut before anyone can see me in my towel... or him.

"It smells like sex in here." He raises an eyebrow.

My face heats. "That wasn't me."

"No?"

"No." I cross my arms.

His gaze drops to my chest, then slowly rises again. A

wicked smile curves his lips, but it slips away. His sudden seriousness makes me straighten.

"Royal Lawson is your brother."

I wince.

He glowers at me. "A detail you failed to mention last night."

"Listen. I don't know you—"

He scoffs.

"I *don't*. All I know is you were using that room to get laid—"

"My room," he interrupts. "I was using my room. You barged into my room."

And you didn't give me any choice once I was inside.

He turns away, drifting over to the made bed. He reaches out, letting his palm coast across the purple bedspread. He reaches my pillow and presses his fingers into it.

"What are you going to tell your brother?"

His back is to me. He's focused more on the pillow and the singular photo I taped to the wall next to it. It's of Royal and me after my high school graduation.

But... what am I going to *tell* him?

"Nothing," I say. "You think I want him finding out about... that?"

He lifts a shoulder and faces me once again. "I don't know what you'd be inclined to share with him."

Is he...

Royal's initial introduction—and subsequent threat to his teammates about me—floats to the front of my mind.

I didn't know this guy was a hockey player, but he obviously is. He lives in the hockey house. He's got the ass of a hockey player. So he's worried about my brother finding out he basically forced himself on me.

Well.

The fact I liked most of it is notwithstanding.

And complicated.

"What will you give me to keep this little secret between us?" The words are out before I can stop him.

His expression sharpens. It's like every bit of him tunes in to me. "What will I *give* you?" His tone is dangerous.

"Yeah."

It's official—I'm losing my mind.

Why am I baiting him?

I don't even know his name.

He steps forward, and I go back. Back, back, back, until I hit the wall. He's right there, and too fast to stop, he tugs my towel.

It loosens and falls to a heap around my feet. I belatedly cover my chest, but he stares only at my face. He leans in. Leans *down*. His lips are inches away.

Is he going to kiss me?

My head moves, tilts back. Waits for him to come just another hair closer.

"I can give you mercy," he breathes. "Or I'll drag you into ruin. Your choice."

5

———

CAMDEN

Ruin.

I'm definitely choosing to fucking ruin her.

Her chest rises and falls too fast. Her eyes fell shut when I brought my face down into hers—not to kiss her, but to watch her reaction. Lips parted, nostrils flaring. If I were to touch her, I bet she'd be just as aroused as last night.

"I'll ruin your reputation," I continue. "Ruin your relationship with your brother. Ruin *you*. You'll never find anyone like me, and that's a goddamn promise."

Her eyes open. Sharp hazel irises bore into mine, and I'm surprised at how she maintains contact. She puts her hand on my chest, her nails flexing slightly and digging into my shirt, then shoves.

I go back a step, and a laugh rumbles through me.

Harper dives for her towel and clutches it to her chest just as her door gives a soft *beep*, and it swings inward.

Her roommate, I'm assuming, stops dead when she sees me.

Then the state of Harper.

Naked, beautiful little thing.

"I—" The roommate stares at me in awe. "You're Camden Church."

I incline my chin. Freaking puck bunny.

"Y-you—"

A guy comes up behind the girl, his hands going to her waist. He does a double take when he sees me, too. Guess he's a hockey fan. *Awkward.*

"Dude. Wow. What an—" He stops when he notices Harper.

I don't want this asshole looking at her naked. The thought sweeps over me, and I block her before I fully consider it. I raise my eyebrow at both of them, and the guy puts it together before his girlfriend.

"We're interrupting," he mumbles. "Dang, sorry, man."

He uses his hold on his girl and drags her backward. The door swings shut, leaving Harper and I alone again.

"Camden Church," she repeats behind my back. "*Church.* What an interesting name."

I whirl around. "What?"

"Camden *Devil* seems more accurate." She smiles tightly at me. "Since you're promising ruin and all that."

Yeah, right. But I'm stuck on how she said my name. Like she hadn't heard it before.

"Did you not know who I was?"

Her hazel eyes widen. Her mouth opens and shuts. Then, the most beautiful laugh trills out of her. Never mind I still have the upper hand. I'm between her and the door, she's *naked* with just a towel clutched to her front, her wet hair trailing water droplets down her chest. She's laughing.

"I'm so sorry, Your Majesty," she finally forces out. "I don't know you. Never heard of Camden Church. Never saw your face—"

"Royal is my best friend." My words come through clenched teeth.

Never mind that my face has been splashed across media outlets all summer. Harper comes from a hockey family, doesn't she? Royal is a great hockey player. He said himself that he watched the draft.

"Does that make you even more special?" She shakes her head and goes to her closet. "He and I don't talk about hockey. I don't like the sport. I certainly don't like the stinky players he's friends with." She glances over her shoulder at me, her hands in her underwear drawer. "That includes you."

This girl.

I haven't felt the emotions buzzing in my chest in a long time. A mix of lust and awe and horror.

If she doesn't know who I am, then what's stopping her from telling Royal? Beyond her own embarrassment. But that will fade, and then the need for revenge will come.

Can't let that happen.

I watch her ignore me. She pulls on underwear, then jeans. Skips the bra and goes straight for a t-shirt, then a heavy sweatshirt. Everything is baggy. She has a killer body—*knew that from the beginning*—but she hides it so thoroughly.

I don't get it.

I don't get her.

But now... I want to know. I need to know.

"Okay." She faces me, hands on her hips. "Are you going to continue to threaten me, or can I go to class?"

I narrow my eyes. "Like that?"

"Yes, *Camden*, this is what I wear."

"You're not wearing makeup."

Her nose wrinkles. "To class?"

"I..." I shake my head. "Never mind."

I feel *beat*. I stride to the door and yank it open, and she slips past me. There's a bag slung over her shoulder. She walks evenly, even though I stick close. I want her to feel I'm following her, and her gait never fucking falters.

Finally, I slow. I let her go on ahead of me, and the puzzle of my best friend's sister only seems to grow more complex. I could spend the time putting it together. Figuring her out.

Or... I could break it and create my own art.

6

HARPER

"Are you dating Camden Church?" My roommate, Cynthia, drops into the chair across from me in the dining hall.

Her boyfriend is close behind—*shocker*. He pulls out the seat beside her, setting down both of their trays.

"Absolutely not." I scoff. "No."

"You—"

"I don't know how you interpreted what you saw, but all that happened was unfortunate timing."

She raises her eyebrows. We're *so* not friends—kind of lost the idea of that happening when I walked in on those two boning—but she's sitting here because she wants gossip fodder. She'll take whatever I say and run to her real friend group, and by breakfast tomorrow, everyone would know.

Even with her proclivity for talking shit, I thought we could get along fine. Enough to survive the semester anyway.

I'm regretting that wholeheartedly.

"Unfortunate timing like, he can't last?"

The feeling of him coming on my face rushes out of the darkness, and my cheeks heat.

"Oh my God," Cynthia squeals. "That's so embarrassing!"

Wait—what? "No—"

She gets up and hurries away, and I'm left staring at the boyfriend. I don't even know his name. He was never introduced. But he winces and shakes his head slowly.

"Stamina problems are the worst. Don't hold it against him—it's more like a compliment." With that, he gathers their food and trails after her.

Oh, no.

Oh shit.

I scramble for my phone.

ME

Mayday! HELP!

I stare at the screen for a long moment, willing my best friend to reply. She's at the neighboring school, St. James University. There's a long-standing rivalry between the two, but I've known Olivia since we were three.

We went to the same daycare and stayed inseparable.

OLIVIA

You've been at that school for 3 days, Harper Marie Shay. What did you do???

Accidentally had a tryst with R's teammate

> And… accidentally insinuated to the gossip queen evil roommate that he's got an excitement issue

What the heck does excitement issue mean??

> Like, uh, coming too early

[laughing crying emoji]

I want to hear this in person

> Ice cream shop in thirty?

Sold.

I MAKE it out of the dining hall unscathed—minus a few strange, pitying looks—and call a car on my phone. My parents were pretty set on the idea of me not having a car while at college. Royal has one, but that's a new development this year. Over the summer, he complained a *lot* about lugging his hockey gear around on foot.

The driver shows up, and I arrive at the ice cream shop situated in St. James U territory just a few minutes before Olivia.

She and I are similar, both in style and temperament. We try not to let people walk all over us, while also retaining wallflower status. It's a fine line to straddle. She wears thick-rimmed glasses, her dark-brown hair is barely wavy and long, with a straight-across bang hiding her forehead. Today, her outfit is comprised of a cream turtleneck sweater under rust-orange overalls and Doc Marten boots. A puffy black coat, hanging open, completes the look.

We hug, and I trail her to the counter.

"How's St. James?" I ask.

She smiles. "It's good. Classes are nice. I've avoided any and all jocks—but honestly, I think they avoid me, too. It's a great system."

"Any hotties in your classes?"

"Just the one." She sighs. "He's so dreamy, Harper. Like, he could be a model for those science magazines. With the lab coats, you know? And the lock of hair that falls down his forehead in a perfect curl. Plus, glasses."

She's going to be a scientist. Not sure what kind—science is *not* my subject—but she's got the brain for it. Plus, the drive.

"Still drooling over him then, huh?" I grin. "Has he noticed you?"

"He complimented my overalls today." She mirrors my expression, but her wide smile drops off faster than mine. "He's so out of my league, it isn't funny."

"You're a steal." I nudge her. "He'd be *lucky* if you gave him a first date."

Olivia rolls her eyes. We order our ice cream and move down to the pick-up window. The shop is *very* clearly SJU branded. Their mascot is a seawolf—whatever the fuck that is—and one is painted across the far wall in the school's colors, burgundy and white. Framingham State U's mascot is a viper, and our colors are purple and black.

I'm not a fan of snakes, but... better than some made-up creature?

"Okay," she says when we have our cups and find a booth in the back of the shop. "Spill."

I tell her everything. From interrupting Cynthia, to Royal's party invite, and his warning to his friends... then walking in on Camden Church fucking some girl. Then her leaving when I *stayed*.

Olivia smacks her palm to her forehead. "You didn't immediately run away?"

"Nope." My face can't get any hotter. "I don't know what's wrong with me. And then..." I quickly relay the rest of it, ending with Camden's visit to my room, his threat, and Cynthia and her boyfriend walking in.

Hate to say *that's* how I learned his name, but... He should've mentioned it.

His reaction to me not knowing, it was kind of funny —and confusing. Like, how big is his ego? To think the whole school knows him automatically?

He's got the equipment to back up the ego...

Nope. Don't think that.

"...and that's when Cynthia assumed I meant his stamina when I said unfortunate timing."

She bursts into laughter. Heads turn in our direction, but she practically howls with it. Tears form in her eyes, and she swipes them away carefully once she regains control.

"Damn, dude." She leans in. "But, like, that kind of sounds a little gray area at the party, right? You didn't..."

I shrug. "I didn't say no. I could've bit his dick off if I didn't want it in my mouth."

Her cheeks pinken. "Right."

"I can't mention this to my brother," I add. "I think he'd actually kill Camden."

Olivia holds up her hand. "You know what we need to do?"

"No..."

"Google." She switches sides in the booth, coming to mine, and pulls up the internet on her phone. I watch her type in Camden's full name, not expecting much.

Instead, dozens of articles, stats, and photos pop up.

My jaw drops.

"He was drafted to the NHL already," she says, pointing at one of the headlines. "This past June."

"Shit."

Guess the ego matches... what, his talent?

My stomach twists.

She clicks around, finally coming up with a highlight reel from the World Juniors championship last year. We have to watch it once through to figure out which one he is, then replay it. I track his number—ninety-six—as he moves across the ice.

He practically floats. It's like dancing, the way the other players seem to be standing still while he twists and dodges around them. And the goalie may as well be caught in molasses, the way he barely reacts to the quick flick of Camden's wrist.

It's beautiful. I know *nothing* about hockey, beyond being dragged to a few of Royal's high school games when they made the playoffs, and here I am, admiring this shit.

Olivia whistles. "That was..."

"I..."

"Yeah." She sets her phone down. "Okay, so. Maybe the rumor won't take. Who would believe that about him anyway?"

"Right."

I've got a bad feeling. It settles in my chest. Every bite of the ice cream lands hard in my stomach. I don't finish it, letting it melt into its cup, and Olivia fills my silence with mindless, easy chatter.

"I should get back," Olivia finally says. "I've got an early class tomorrow and some work to finish."

"Yeah. It was good to see you." I hug her, my eyes closing when her arms tighten around my back. "Wish me luck."

"Good luck."

"Thanks."

I'm gonna need it.

7

———

CAMDEN

She's spreading rumors about me.

Royal doesn't know it's her. The whispers are kind enough to leave her name out of the equation. It's just *my* name that's taking the brunt of it.

Stamina problems.

In other words: blowing my load too early.

What the fuck? Where did she even come up with that?

Half my teammates are sympathetic. They don't believe it—not to my face anyway. Royal snickered when he showed me the post on social media, and the comments from girls about how *sad* that was, but he stopped when my expression went blank.

Because I was waiting for the other shoe to drop—*Harper*—and when it didn't, I snatched his phone and scrolled through the comments.

Some said maybe I just needed practice. One suggested I just *really* liked the girl. Or she had some secret talents that made me come in my pants.

In my *pants?*

As if.

I ride with Royal back to the house. We park beside another teammate's huge truck, on the far side, and we grab our hockey gear out of the trunk. He slings his bag over his shoulder, stick in hand, and heads for the front porch.

"What are you doing here?" he asks someone.

I slam the trunk shut and follow, only to stop dead.

And luckily, Royal misses my reaction. His back is to me.

Harper sits on the steps of the porch. Her dark-blond hair is loose around her shoulders, and she's wearing the same clothes from earlier. The black sweatshirt, the jeans that don't hug her legs in the slightest. It's like she's allergic to stuff that fits her.

She rises, and her gaze moves from her brother to me. Then quickly back to him.

"My roommate is being a bitch." Her voice rings out across the lawn. "We had a misunderstanding. Argued about it. I was just going to sit at my desk, but then her boyfriend came in..."

My jaw clenches.

"They know you're not comfortable with sex," Royal says, just barely audible. "She's using it against you."

Harper lifts her chin. "I'm not a prude."

"Of course not." Royal gestures. "Let's go inside. You can hang out. Spend the night. Whatever you want."

She lets out a sigh and accepts his offered hand. He pulls her to her feet and guides her onto the porch ahead of him. The door is already unlocked, our other two roommates having arrived already.

She's his sister.

His younger sister.

I should not be thinking about her pussy. Or her mouth. Or her nipples.

Gah.

"The only way the roommate won't run her off is if she stands her ground," I blurt out. "Maybe she should just go back."

Royal glares at me. "Seriously?"

I lift my shoulder. "What?"

"Not helpful, asshole."

I press my lips together. She takes a seat in the living room, at one end of the couch, and Royal and I both go upstairs to drop our bags in our rooms. Royal heads down the hall and disappears into the bathroom.

I go downstairs.

She's on her phone, scrolling with her lower lip caught between her teeth.

"You think you're clever?"

Her head jerks up.

I approach and stand over her. "You think being *here*, close to him, will protect you?"

"No. I just don't have anywhere else to go." She pushes off the couch, rising, and our chests brush. She has to tilt her head back to meet my gaze. "Your *problem* isn't mine."

"My only problem is you." I lean into her slightly. The feel of her breasts pressing through the fabric between us is... enjoyable. Distracting. "And if you're a prude, then I'm a saint."

Her expression flashes. Anger, then suddenly, calm. Stoicism.

At the sound of footsteps on the stairs, I take a large step back. I move around her and go into the kitchen. I adjust my dick in my pants, instantly annoyed it woke up for her. I busy myself in the fridge, searching for something to occupy my brain and hands.

Royal enters, and I glance over.

Calculating.

"This roommate of hers seems like a bitch," I say.

He frowns. "You just said she should work it out. Stand her ground or whatever."

"Yeah, well." I shrug. "Maybe you just offer your baby sister the extra room."

It's at the back of the house, it's small, and it only has one window. The others all have at least two, and they've got more breathing space. The owner of the house, who leases it to us through the school, didn't want to deal with someone complaining about it.

But technically, it has a closet. It's considered a bedroom.

"Maybe," he hedges. "Not sure I want her around you heathens."

I roll my eyes.

"It's not you I worry about," he assures me. "It's everyone else."

That doesn't make me feel shitty or anything. I grab a beer and toss it to him.

"I've got a paper to work on before I pass out," I say. "Have fun babysitting."

He scoffs, but I'm already gone.

I HAD A FIFTY-FIFTY SHOT, and tonight, the odds are in my favor.

Royal has passed out on the couch, and his sister is, presumably, tucked away in his bedroom. I make sure he's actually asleep, listening for the deep sounds of his almost-snores, then tiptoe back upstairs.

I open his door and step inside.

Close it behind me.

Lock it, just to be safe.

I can blame it on Harper if I need to. The blinds are shut, but little dots of warm light from the street come in and create a path across the bed. Across Harper's bare leg. One is on top of the blankets, the other hidden under it.

She's on her stomach. The bare knee is brought up on her side.

My heartbeat picks up speed. I approach and climb on the bed, hovering over her. She's in panties and a t-shirt.

She doesn't wake up at the dip in the mattress.

Like this, her lips parted, her breathing slow and even, she seems too peaceful.

She's a beautiful little butterfly, wings wet from emerging from her cocoon, and I am the spider.

All at once, I drop my weight onto her. My hips press

to her ass, my knee keeps her calf from sliding down. My dick goes stiff immediately. I run my hands up her arms, finding her wrists. Holding them down.

And my mouth finds her ear.

She startles awake, and at the first thrash, I sink my teeth into the shell of her ear.

She stills.

"You've got some instinct, after all," I breathe. "Pity, I was hoping for more of a fight."

It takes me saying it to realize it. I want her to fight me. I want her angry eyes. I want to *make her*.

"Now we're going to find out if last night was a fluke," I continue. "If the voyeurism did you in, or *me*."

I release one of her wrists and trail my fingers down her side, shifting my weight just enough to get between our bodies. I yank her panties aside and run my finger down her center, and I smile at the wetness that awaits me.

"Stop," she says in a low voice. "My brother—"

"Is asleep downstairs. And even if he comes up, the door is locked." I nip her ear again, and she shudders against me. "Will you yell out to him when he jiggles the knob? Will you pray he puts a stop to this? Only for him to break down the door and see you come on my cock?"

She fights me harder. Her head lifts, knocking into my chin, and I raise my head out of the way. I snicker and withdraw farther, until I'm knelt between her parted legs.

I shove my sweatpants and boxers down and wrap my hand around my cock. I find the condom I brought with me and take a moment to roll it on. There's some deeper temptation to forego it entirely, to *feel* her...

Maybe another time.

"Up on your knees," I order softly. "Head in the pillow."

She rolls on her back and kicks at me. Her heel lands in my abdomen, and I grunt. I catch her foot and yank.

She slides across the bed. Her other leg comes up, and I manage to grab her ankle. I rise, holding both. I put her calves together, banding my arm around them. Her ass lifts off the bed.

"That the position you wanted?" I tug at her panties, moving the pesky strip hiding her cunt from me.

She pushes at my shoulder, her nails scraping my neck.

"I don't think you actually want me to stop." I lean forward, practically folding her in half. My cock is so hard, it pulses with an ache to be inside her. "Otherwise, you'd be yelling your head off."

There's an idea. Somewhere isolated. Somewhere I can elicit sweet screams from her.

Her gaze moves to the ceiling.

It's answer enough. She keeps her hand on my arm. I adjust her legs on my shoulder and line up at her slit.

As I push into her.

Her eyes roll back.

She's tight. Her muscles grip at my length. Every inch I give her causes a shudder to flutter through her abdomen. I groan through my teeth at the sensation. Halfway, I pull out, then push deeper. Her back arches.

I shove her shirt up, exposing her breasts.

Her nipples pebble.

Fuck me twice.

Finally, I sink all the way inside her. I stay there for a long moment, adjusting to her heat, to the squeeze of her cunt. I palm her breast and pinch her nipple.

"Look at me." I wait. Pinch again.

Her gaze comes back.

Her hand falls away from my arm, and instead tangles in the blankets at her side. Her other one moves up and braces against the headboard.

It's like... I've caught her, and now she's willing?

"You like being thoroughly trapped, hmm?" I draw out slowly, then slide in. "You like there's no choice in this? You fight, I fuck you hard. You go still... maybe I make you come, too."

Her lips part. She considers, but I have no fucking idea what's going on in that brain of hers. When she doesn't say anything else, I move. My hips jack, and before long, my pace quickens.

Stamina issues, my ass.

My fingers find her clit. She gasps, the sound sharp in the quiet. I work her toward the edge. Her body sways with every thrust. I can't stop staring at her breasts, and the need to suck her nipple into my mouth, to bite and suck, is almost overwhelming.

I fight it off and focus on the rest. Her smooth calves, her ankles next to my ear. The soft rolls of her belly in this position.

Does she wear the oversized clothing to hide that? The extra padding on her thighs?

It's unnecessary. She feels more real than any stick-thin bottle-blonde I've had before.

"Better come quietly," I goad. "Or wake the whole house up—then see what happens."

She twists, her mouth opening. Nothing comes out. No scream, no gasp or whimper. But her cunt suddenly tightens, clenching around me, and I'm the one to hiss out a breath. It's too much, and I only last another minute. Just when the pulsing inside her eases, I erupt.

I withdraw and drop her legs. She curls on her side for a long moment, then climbs off the bed. Her hair is a mess. Strands have escaped the tie she must've put in to sleep, hanging around her face. Carefully, she tucks them behind her ears.

Condom removed, I tie it and hoist my sweatpants and boxers back into place.

"I suppose your kink is that you don't get a choice in the matter." I tilt my head. It's hard to make out her expression in the light. "Do you feel dirtier for it? That you gave in, in the end? Same as last night. You accepted it the second my cock passed your lips."

She looks away.

I smile, but my insides are writhing. It hits me that I like this, too. The girls who throw themselves at me are boring. They're tired clichés. But Harper, off-limits, forbidden Harper... she's fascinating.

"You truly can't escape me now."

8

HARPER

Olivia and I enter the arena with no small amount of trepidation. I've said it before, but I'll say it again: just because my brother plays hockey doesn't mean I follow it. And this will be my first time attending one of his home games as a student, sitting amongst *our* peers. Not just his—mine. Which is arguably the most nerve-wracking part of this whole thing.

I'd much rather be sitting in her dorm room, watching *The Breakfast Club* for the eightieth time, than be here. What can I say? It's a timeless classic.

But Cynthia had some cheerleading meeting come up, she had already got a ticket from the Student Center and asked if I knew anyone who would use it. So I grabbed a ticket for myself, and now Olivia and I are at a hockey game.

She borrowed one of my FSU sweatshirts. I stole one of Royal's hoodies that has his name on the sleeve.

It's been three days since I stayed at the hockey house.

Three days since I've seen Camden Church.

And for three days, I've struggled to wrap my mind around him. And what he did.

As soon as he left, I opened the window and let in the chill fall breeze. It smelled like sex in Royal's room, and I didn't know how I would explain it if he came in. Which, according to Camden, would be a horrible, terrible thing.

For him.

But also for me, if his threats are to be believed.

In the end, it didn't matter. I cleaned up, stared at my pale face in the mirror, contemplated showering to rid myself of the sensation of his touch, then eventually gave up and went to bed. Royal never came up, and when I crept out in the morning—sheets changed on his bed like a nice sister—he was still asleep.

The hairs on the back of my neck stand up. I glance around the arena at the mouth to our section. Only a small portion of the stands are filled in so far, and no one is looking at me. My gaze coasts over the rink full of players warming up, and I pause on one player.

Helmet on, cage obscuring his features, but it's very clearly Camden. He's looking in my direction. Assuming he's looking at me would be laughable.

I shake it off and take my seat with Olivia. The rumors about him died out relatively fast. It never spread farther than student social media, which is good. No need for the NHL media to catch wind of a... prank.

A misunderstanding, more like.

The horn blows, and the players leave the ice. The Zamboni comes on, along with two students who remove the goals and push them out of the path.

I fiddle with my sleeve. Then my nails. Olivia goes to get us popcorn, and I sink lower in my seat. We're about to be surrounded by FSU students. I keep my legs angled out of the way, and my row fills out, along with the ones around me.

No one pays me any mind.

The good news is, I'm an unknown on campus. No one has connected me to Royal, besides a few teammates who heard our introductions at that party. Tomorrow morning, they're all getting on a bus for an away game tomorrow night. A fan bus has been arranged to take students over to Crown Point University, which is a four-hour drive from here.

Nothing sounds worse than a four-hour drive in a cramped bus full of preening girls hoping to get laid by the star players. Plus, a four-hour drive *home* after the game.

No thanks.

A chill goes down my back. I rub my arms and glance around again, just as my phone vibrates in my pocket.

ROYAL

You at the game?

> Yeah, grabbed tickets last minute.
> That ok?

Of course.

> Good luck x

He doesn't reply, and I tuck it away again. By the time Olivia returns with popcorn and drinks, the opening ceremony is beginning. The main lights dim, while spot-lights dance over the crowd and the ice. We stand at the edge of the student section, which is going nuts for the players about to burst out from the locker room.

Their opening music swells, and the visceral excite-ment of the people around me almost chokes me. Echoing *boos* fill the arena when the opposing team makes their appearance.

Finally, our players skate out and the arena goes crazy. The whole team skates a few laps, then lines up on the goal line. The cheers turn to boos when the other team appears on the ice.

The announcer calls the home team's starting lineup. A video plays along on the screen, and my breath catches when Camden appears. He smirks at the camera. Royal is next, crossing his arms as the camera pans around him. He looks confident. Almost a stranger.

Once the announcer is done, the lights come back on. Those not starting go to their benches. One national anthem later, and the game begins.

My brother plays defense, and he leans over with his stick at the ready, positioned between the face-off and his goalie. The ref skates up to the two players in the middle of the red center circle.

He drops the puck, there's a flurry of motion, and I lose track of it almost immediately. The players have no problem following it, though. The other team—in white jerseys with red lettering—get it back in their zone. They seem to take a minute to collect themselves, then attack.

It's fast-paced, and the way the players crash into the boards makes my heart skip. Especially when it's Royal—

either doing the hitting or taking it—but he seems fine every time. He steals the puck from an opposing player and passes it to Camden. It's so fast, the puck slaps against the blade of his stick with a *crack*.

Camden takes it toward the goal, dodging around an incoming player like we saw him do in the highlight reel, and veer toward the goal. An SVU player dives.

I jerk, wincing, and Camden somehow avoids him. He goes airborne, the puck seeming to keep with him, and he's all alone on the ice.

Shoot—*score*.

The horn blows. The crowd around us leaps to their feet. Olivia and I belatedly follow. It was so fast... I don't know how anyone even followed that, let alone a goalie having a chance at stopping it.

"Holy shit." Olivia laughs. "That was epic!"

I stare down at the ice. Camden is swarmed by his teammates, their celebratory huddle brief. He takes off from the pack first, going down his bench line and bumping his glove with the rest of the team. The spotlights flash around again, music blaring.

Around us, people high-five, bump fists.

The game passes in a blur. One period blends into two, and at one point I look up, shocked to see there's only two minutes left of the third period. The score is 4-1 in favor of Framingham State U.

Good.

Great, even.

The final seconds count down, the buzzer sounds, and we all scream and cheer as the home team jumps out onto the ice. I imagine the team will be celebrating tonight, which means I can spend another night free of Camden.

Rather, free of worrying Camden is going to do something.

It doesn't matter. None of that matters.

I grab Olivia's hand and pull her up the steps along with the crowd. We get into the hallway, and everyone heads in the same direction.

"Harper!" a guy calls.

I stop dead in my tracks. Olivia crashes into me from behind, sending me stumbling forward. It takes a long moment for the crowd to open up, revealing the body attached to the voice.

Max Keegan.

Olivia's grip on my hand tightens, crushing my fingers.

She knows him, too.

He comes toward us decked out in red. The opposing team's colors. Shadow Valley University is written across his chest in black lettering. He dodges around people, and Olivia yanks me backward. We reach the wall, and the flood of people stops moving all around us. They just stream in front, with our backs to the wall.

But he still approaches.

"Wow." He stops a foot away, and that feels *too close.*

My breath catches. "What are you doing here?"

He squints, confusion flickering across his expression. Like he can't imagine why I'm asking. "I go to Shadow Valley. I came as a fan."

"I—"

"I love hockey," he continues. "I used to play, remember?"

Olivia is going to break my hand with her death grip. But I think I'm squeezing back just as hard. He looks the same but different. Taller, if that's possible? His sandy-blond hair is styled. The sweatshirt, clinging to his biceps, is fitted around his torso. It shows off what he's proud of—his strength, his fitness, his *size*.

All that is familiar. The squareness of his jaw, his dark eyes. The way his lips flatten when people say things he doesn't like, but just for a split second. Like a tic, or a twitch.

Seeing him is like seeing a ghost.

Terrible. Impossible.

"Y-you love—"

"Hockey," he finishes. His smile is bland. "And obviously the chance to see Royal in action couldn't be passed up. But seeing *you*? This has got to be fate, Harper. I had no idea you decided to go to FSU."

Olivia shifts, putting herself a little in front of me. "You're not playing for Shadow Valley then, Max?"

Disgust flashes across his expression. "No. Knee injury ruled me out, unfortunately. No matter—it was a stupid high school dream."

"Shame," Olivia murmurs. "Well... we've got to get going. Meeting friends, you know. It was good to see you."

He looks at me, and I barely suppress a shudder.

I can't find any words that will get me out of this situation, but Olivia isn't allowing room for Max's doubt. She tows me away from him with a casual, backward wave.

We weave through the crowd. It's only when we're around a corner and Olivia murmurs the all clear that I take a gasping breath.

It's not enough—my chest aches. I can't seem to inhale enough. The closeness of the crowd only adds to the overwhelm. Light spots flicker in my peripheral vision.

"I'm going to pass out," I say as loud as I can.

Ahead of me, Olivia swears. We take a turn, go through a door, and the noise, the crowd, it all goes quiet. There's a stairwell in front of us, and she guides me down a step, then another, and presses on my shoulders.

I fold, sitting hard on the stairs. There's an elephant on my chest.

"It's okay." She cups my cheek. "Breathe slow. After me. Inhale... ah, *fuck*."

My hearing goes first.

Then my vision.

Then, I suppose, everything else.

9

HARPER

"Are you sure?"

I shudder, and aches make themselves known along my back. My arms. My head pounds.

"Who is he?" another voice asks.

I open my eyes.

Royal and Olivia stand over me, but they didn't ask the question.

Camden Church is behind my brother, a few steps down. Standing, he's even with my seated position. He's the one who inquired, and Royal and Olivia both twist to eye him.

"No one." Olivia's tone dismisses him.

He bristles.

"An old teammate of mine," Royal says on a sigh.

I lick my lips. That's not the whole story—not even close. Maybe Royal wants to keep his best friend at a distance from this? For me? It wouldn't help—Camden is about as close as someone can get, whether I want him here or not.

Not in an entirely bad way.

Not like Max Keegan.

"He had a thing for me."

Camden's gaze never leaves mine, even when his best friend is speaking, but now a muscle in his jaw spasms at my words.

Royal grimaces.

"He would leave flowers in my room," I continue. "When we weren't home. I'd come back from some after-school activity, or a sleepover, and find pink roses spread across my bed. He always talked about going away to school, though. I thought when he graduated with Royal, that was the end of it..."

"Was it?" Camden asks.

"No."

He scowls. "So, what, he just showed up?"

Olivia takes over. "He was wearing Shadow Valley gear. Said he just wanted to see Royal play and didn't expect Harper to be here."

Max is the reason I don't post on social media. He's the reason I didn't make it known to anyone outside of Olivia and Royal where I had chosen to go to school. My parents have been worried about it so much that they got the local police involved, but with no imminent threat...

Flowers don't count, I guess. They did put in a report with the police about the breaking and entering, but that's where it stopped. They couldn't prove it was him. He was never on the security cameras we put up, there were no fingerprints.

I didn't even know it *was* him until he asked if I got his gift.

"Now he knows she's here," Camden muses. He eyes Royal and lifts a brow.

My brother seems to come to some sort of decision. About me, I would imagine. I open my mouth to argue, but he beats me to the punch.

"No," he snaps. "Don't. There's an extra room in the hockey house, and it's yours until further notice. This is not an option, Harper."

I gape at him. Olivia even seems surprised.

"You can't be serious." I grip the railing and haul myself up. "I'm not moving in with you and four other guys."

He shakes his head. "It's that or I tell our parents."

Ah, shit.

There's no way they'd let me stay if they knew Max had been here.

Olivia shifts her weight, and I can read her mind. She's thinking, *well, it's not the worst idea.* The one thing Max always shied away from was fucking with Royal. They were teammates, after all.

"Come on." Royal holds out his hand. "We can use the exit downstairs. Then we're packing your shit."

I heave a sigh, but what am I to do? Wait for Max to break into my dorm room? The security in that place is shy of nothing. Camden was able to get in easily. Cynthia would probably believe whatever story Max fed her about me and let him wait for me on my bed.

I wrinkle my nose at that thought.

But in the end, I take my brother's hand.

"THIS IS IT." Royal gestures.

One of the other guys in the house, Lucas, is kneeling next to a half-inflated air mattress in my new room. The whir of the motor pumping it almost overtakes Royal's words. Other than the air mattress, the room is empty.

No dresser, no lighting except the glaring overhead one. That'll need to be changed immediately. Well, tomorrow. It's late now, and there are less people filling the downstairs of the hockey house than I was expecting.

Maybe the party is elsewhere?

"Why do you guys call it the hockey house when there's only four of you living here?"

Lucas snorts. He's a defenseman like Royal, I think. I don't know much else about him; beyond that he has the vibe of a Canadian hockey player. I can't explain it.

"It became the hangout spot for the starters. Hosted a few parties here, then the name stuck," he explains. "A lot of the other guys either live in dorms or apartments around Framingham, but this is the biggest."

Huh.

Well, that's dumb.

Once the air mattress is finished inflating, he shuts off the motor, caps it, and scoots past us. "Welcome to the house, roomie."

Royal glares at his back, then tows me farther into the room. He shakes out a fitted sheet and spreads it across the mattress. I have a laundry basket full of blankets and pillows, and we make the bed in silence.

Lucas comes up a minute later with my two suitcases.

"You pack bricks in here, Lawson?" he grunts.

"Shay," I correct. "Harper Shay."

"Right. *Shay.*"

"And, as a matter of fact... no. It's just a lot of clothing." And shoes. And my textbooks, notebooks, and pen case. They wouldn't all fit in my backpack, so...

The textbooks are probably the problem.

"Thanks for your help."

He waves me off and heads out again. Royal plants his hands on his hips, staring around at the not-quite-so-empty room.

"Shopping tomorrow," he says. "We'll get everything you need."

"You have a game tomorrow," I point out. "You leave early. You should already be asleep—"

"I'll sleep on the bus," he interrupts. "I'll leave you a credit card, yeah? Don't make that face. It's fine. I just want to make sure you're settled."

"I just need sleep," I say quietly. "The rest... Olivia and I will figure it out tomorrow."

He nods, then pauses. Carefully, he shuts the door and faces me. He seems a lot more tired than he did a minute ago, like a mask has dropped. "I'm just worried about you. I know you wanted to go farther away for school, and FSU wasn't exactly your idea. But Olivia is close, and I'm here, so..."

"I know."

A lump forms in my throat. I *was* planning on going farther away. But after everything with Max last year, even when *he* was supposedly off at college, it began to feel dangerous going somewhere new. Somewhere I'd be all alone.

"I'm glad you're here. Playing kick-ass hockey with

your friends." I make a shooing motion. "Now go away so I can get some sleep."

He chuckles, but he does leave me. I hesitate for a second, then lock the door behind him. I kick off my shoes and flop onto the bed. My phone vibrates against my ass. I roll and pull it from my jeans, and I freeze.

UNKNOWN

It was really good seeing you, Harper. I look forward to our next run-in.

10

CAMDEN

I'm playing a drinking game.

Every time Royal mentions the high school stalker, I take a shot.

So far, I'm winning. Or losing, maybe. There's a small group of us—mainly hockey players and the girls they kept from leaving with their friends—in the living room. The bottle of whiskey is propped on my leg, and I've got a shot glass in the other.

I think I've taken three? No, four.

Four shots in the last twenty minutes.

Harper is upstairs. Royal took her straight up when we all got back—minus Harper's friend, who said she'd see her tomorrow—and I stayed down here. Of course I stayed instead of following her. Him.

Her.

She's an addiction I am struggling to fight, and the fact she's upstairs again is boring a hole in my head.

"He's just an overstepping, waste-of-space human

being," Royal spits. "I should've killed him when I had the chance."

Royal saying he'd kill someone is comical. He'd never.

Maybe not *never*. But... he probably wouldn't go out and plan it. It would have to be impulsive. An act of anger, maybe? Which, clearly, this Max guy has gotten under his skin.

I shake my head and pour another shot. I spill a little on my pants, grimace, then swallow down the liquid anyway. It barely burns. In fact, it's starting to taste more like water than alcohol.

I'm not a lightweight, but we have a game tomorrow. I should quit while I'm ahead and go to bed. It's approaching midnight, which means we're approaching the start of my pre-game routine.

Step one: Go to my room by midnight, if not earlier.

Step two: Strip to boxers, get in bed, listen to fifteen minutes of classical piano.

I don't usually make it past the first piece in my playlist. I've always been blessed with falling asleep quickly.

Tomorrow morning, I'll get up, go for a light jog, eat a protein-and-carb breakfast, shower, and report to the arena for our bus departure at ten-something. Since there's no morning practice scheduled at our arena, we'll get straight on the road. Naps are acceptable. We'll practice at the rink in Crown Point, check in to our hotels, and basically be free until we need to be back for the game.

Easy.

Well—it's easy because it's mapped out.

I did the same thing yesterday, minus the shots. Went to bed, listened to my music. Got up for morning skate, had a good breakfast. Went to class, napped, then played.

Now I'm considering *not* doing that.

Now... I'm considering going upstairs, bypassing my room, and finding my way into Harper's. It's a bad idea. Terrible, even. But I cannot explain the feeling that went through me when Royal got a call from Harper's friend, and his face went white.

They've been dealing with a stalker.

I glower at the whiskey bottle. No one should be stalking her, but I do understand the impulse. The craving to follow her around, to learn every inch of her patterns...

I set the bottle and shot glass aside and rise abruptly.

"Sorry, guys. I'm headed up." I wave and leave the room fast. My only pit stop is for a chilled bottle of water, and then I'm safe in my room.

Free of the temptation of Harper Shay.

I pop back out into the bathroom, and I'm in my room before my phone ticks over to midnight. I strip and lie flat, put on the playlist with its sleep timer, and shimmy until I can get fully comfortable.

My mind buzzes on whiskey and thoughts of Harper. I take my time imagining how she looked in all the different times I've seen her. At the party, in this very room—leaving her scent of arousal in her wake—and later, at her dorm. Her naked body.

Bad Church, I chastise.

She didn't scream. She fought, but she didn't... She didn't really mind it all that much.

It's the whiskey in my blood telling me she *liked* it.

I could prove she likes it.

The music shuts off, and my eyes open in the darkness.

I never stay awake long enough for it to turn off.

Routine broken.

I fling the blankets off my legs and stand. In the darkness, I pick my way to my door and crack it open. Voices downstairs filter up, and it takes a second, but then Royal's separates. He's talking about Shadow Valley, which is an adjacent topic to the stalker. He could go on for a while with his hostages.

I mean, teammates.

Better he be downstairs, occupied, than already in his room and in danger of intercepting me on his way to the bathroom.

No, the hallway is empty and dark.

At Harper's door, I reach up and feel along the top of the doorframe. There's a long, thin nail there, ready and waiting. We put it there once when someone accidentally locked the door on their way out, and I learned how to pick it.

It just requires a little *pop.*

And then it gives. The knob turns easily under my palm, and I slip into the darkened room. I close and lock the door behind me and take stock.

There are shitty blinds on the single window, doing nothing to stop the full streetlight from flooding in. Harper is splayed out on an air mattress in the middle of the room.

As much as I want this for just me, something else,

darker, wants to ensure she won't do anything crazy—like tell her brother. Which means I need to collect dirt on her. Something to smear her name just as surely as she'd hurt mine.

My hand goes to my pocket. To my phone in it.

I pull it out and set the shutter timing. Technology these days can make a dark room seem well lit. It used to be old, fancy cameras that could be manipulated like that. Now, the everyday cell phone can handle it, too.

I hold steady as the little bar on the bottom runs, taking the photo. And, sure enough, Harper's features are clear. Shadowy, somewhat mysterious, but good enough.

Will she wake up? The thrill of not knowing rolls through me, and I peel the blankets off her legs. Pausing, waiting. There's no change in her breathing, she doesn't shift. Her face remains relaxed, her lips parted.

Perfect.

Hate and lust roll through me. She's fucking with me, even when she's asleep. Just being in this house—just being *her*. I take a breath, then go for her sleep shorts. I maneuver them off her body and toss them to the floor.

Her panties can shift aside.

I take another photo, then set my phone on the windowsill. I angle it so her face can't be seen. The neck down, though, seems like fair game. Her breasts, her nipples visible through the thin fabric of her t-shirt.

I hit *record*, then circle around. If I keep my angle right, I won't be in the frame either. I'll just be an anonymous body fucking another anonymous body.

I spread her legs and climb over her, my gaze trained on her face.

Still sleeping.

Still peaceful.

"You are the temptation that will kill me," I whisper.

And yet, my cock is hard. I push my boxers down, slide the strip of damp fabric between her legs out of the way, and guide my tip to her wet entrance. I thrust into her carefully, inch by inch. I feed her my dick slower than I've ever had to do, but there's part of me that now doesn't want her to wake up.

I like a challenge.

And fucking Harper while she sleeps, leaving her with only the feeling of being ravaged, with cum leaking from her cunt, sings in my blood.

That's what I want.

No—that's what I fucking need.

If she wakes up, I'll try again tomorrow. Maybe I'll drug her. Or put my hand at her throat, my fingers digging into her pulse points, until she passes back out.

This infatuation with her is insane. It doesn't make sense.

And yet—

I let out a low groan when I bottom out inside her.

She scared away the girl I was screwing—*mid-screw*—and she didn't bat an eye. She listens to my orders, even as she glares at me. She fights but she likes it when I win.

Where else am I going to find that?

My muscles tense, but I keep myself hovering off of her. I don't want the weight of my body to wake her. Our only point of contact is where I'm inside her. The brush of my hips against hers. The barest touch of her calves against my knees.

Then, I begin.

I take what I need from her body, every move sending a tremor through my abdomen and up my back. She doesn't offer any resistance, but the faint pulse of arousal in her cunt seems to echo straight up my dick.

She gets wetter.

"You better be dreaming about me," I growl under my breath.

She squeezes around me.

I'm too far gone to stop. Her face doesn't change. Her chest rises and falls steadily. But her pussy seems to have a mind of its own, the flutter of muscles inside her tipping me over the edge faster than I expect.

Pleasure zings through my cock, up my back. I see stars for a minute, and my hearing goes out. It's replaced by a rushing noise that takes over, only to fade a minute later.

I fucked her without a condom. My cum is inside her.

Harper still sleeps.

I pull out and slip off the mattress, and she rolls onto her side. She brings her knees up, exposing the wet spot on her panties.

My cum, her arousal.

I exhale slowly, then smile. I go to retrieve my phone and end the recording.

Only time will tell if this needs to work its way into my new routine.

11

HARPER

I wake with my hand in my underwear. My fingers press to my clit, my hips shift and roll. I let out an unholy moan and twist onto my stomach, unable to fight the urge to bring myself to orgasm. It's instinct, and it doesn't take me long to tip over the edge.

I groan into my pillow, mouth open, the fabric smothering the noise.

The sensation drifts away, and I sag.

Can't say I've had that happen too many times.

The air mattress held up surprisingly well overnight. Once my muscles aren't jelly, I fling myself off and into a standing position. My toes hit my shorts, and I pause.

I went to sleep with them on. I always do.

Jeez. Was I so horny I pushed them off?

My face heats, and I quickly put them back on. I grab my phone and scan it, and a chill runs through me. I never opened the text from the unknown number last night, and it still stares at me from my lock screen.

I blocked Max's number after graduation, half

convinced I'd never see him again. It didn't matter that he didn't leave. *I* was leaving. My friends back home knew to keep their mouths shut, and everyone else didn't matter.

Running into him at the game was a worst-case-scenario situation I had never even prepared for. Of course, the number that texted me is totally different from the one I still have blocked. Did he get a new one so he could contact me again?

A new text comes in, but this one is welcome.

ROYAL

House is yours. Doors are locked. We'll be back on the bus after the game… should get in pretty late.

Don't suck tonight

I smile and drop the phone back to the bed, refusing to think any more about Max Keegan. Even if he knows I now attend Framingham State, he doesn't know where I live. He can wander campus, but I'm not there.

I'm safe.

And an empty house means I can gather my clothes, towel, and toiletries and walk to the bathroom in the hallway in my sleep stuff. No worrying about running into my brother's teammates and them getting the wrong idea.

I have curves. I'm not going to lie about that. I know what it feels like to have a guy make eye contact, then his gaze just… drops to my chest.

They're not subtle.

It's already awkward, knowing Royal probably didn't

give Lucas and Connor, the last roommate, a choice on the matter. Lucas didn't seem put out. I have yet to come face-to-face with Connor, beyond passing him on my way out the door.

Then, of course, there's Camden Church.

No need to guess how he feels about me being here.

Arms full, I nudge the bathroom door shut and set my stuff down on the counter. As far as bathrooms go, this one could definitely be better. Or worse.

I flick on the switch for the light and the fan, and frown when something flutters on the mirror.

There's a folded piece of paper taped to it.

I lock the door and gently pull it off. If it's not for me, then I can just put it back. But there is an H scrawled on the front...

Who's leaving me notes?

I unfold it and scan the handwriting, and my stomach flips.

> Thanks for the content, Harper. The WatchMe subscription I started in your name is already going viral. You moving in is the best thing to happen to my bank account. Minus the NHL contract, obviously.
>
> —C

WHAT?

I reread it, but it's not comprehending. WatchMe is a site for people to post erotic stuff. Pictures, videos, that sort of thing. Sex.

C is very obviously Camden. But he wouldn't...

I scramble back to my room and grab my phone. I go to the website and search my full name, and my stomach drops when I get a hit.

My face.

My name.

A bio I most certainly did not write about how I'm adventurous and like trying exotic stuff. *Excuse me?* Bile rises up my throat, and I swallow sharply. I scroll down.

There's a public photo posted.

I can't look at it.

I have to. Don't want to, but...

It's like a train wreck. Or a car crash you pass on the highway. An ugly one, with glass on the road and maybe a burning engine. Pieces of the cars littered all over the asphalt. It leaves you questioning how it happened, if the people are okay—and knowing, deep down, they're probably not.

So even though I should close out of it, I look closer.

My anger comes swift and hot. It's not of me in my dorm or crashing in Royal's bed the night of that party—or even in Camden's room when he fucked my mouth. I wouldn't have been surprised if he had a camera set up with the previous girl, then left it running when I interrupted.

Nope. This is a whole new level.

This was *last night*. The near-empty room, the air

mattress—*me*, sleeping, my underwear kind of sucked into my ass crack a bit, revealing my cheeks.

I tilt my head and zoom in. There's a decent number of details in the low light...

Okay, no, stop.

I cannot think he got a quality shot. I like photography—always messed around with a camera when I was in high school, then signed up for a class at FSU—and have been studying how to improve my craft.

Not that I've ever entered into the realm of what could be classified as boudoir. Maybe. My interest lies more in portraits. Faces. Especially the unaware ones.

I suppose this qualifies. Is that why something flutters in my chest, and not entirely in a bad way?

Because seriously, did he edit that? On what program?

Oh my God. What is *wrong* with me?!

He posted that without my permission. He opened a whole account under my name *without my permission.*

I click on the caption, and the nausea returns.

HAD A LATE-NIGHT VISITOR... don't worry, we caught it on camera. ;) Premiering only for subscribers tonight at 10 p.m.!

THERE ARE FOUR HUNDRED LIKES.

Four hundred people saw that post. The photo.

I fall to my knees in front of the toilet. My stomach

cramps, and I squeeze my eyes shut as I throw up whatever was left in my stomach.

This is too much.

Too far.

And the worst part? He's gone. It'll be done and posted by the time he gets back from the game, and I can't do anything except watch it happen.

Olivia and I sit on her bed in her St. James University dorm room. I'm wrapped in layers of blankets, around my back and up to the top of my head like a hood to shield me. A bowl of popcorn sits in my lap, and only one hand is unswathed to make the journey from the kernels to my mouth.

The Breakfast Club plays on her laptop, but I don't think either of us are watching it.

Instead, we're focused on my phone.

I made a dummy account out of sheer desperation— regrettably paying four dollars to subscribe to my own page—and now we wait for the notification of a new post.

Ten o'clock approaches slowly, as if time knows what we're waiting for and is dragging its heels. Every minute feels like five.

This morning, I brushed my teeth again to erase the taste of stomach bile, showered, and practically sprinted out of the empty house. I called for a ride, and it took me to St. James University, where I wandered until I found Olivia's dorm.

The mood to shop at the mall or local thrift stores

never appeared. Instead, I burst into tears as soon as Olivia opened her door, and she decided we were hunkering down on her campus all day.

I used her laptop to order a set of hangers, which will be delivered in two days. If I survive that long. We went to the library, hung out in the student center, and then made our way back to her room, where we now anxiously await ten o'clock.

The best thing that could've happened for the two of us was Olivia scoring a single room.

No nasty, sex-having roommate to kick her out.

Cynthia caused all this in the first place. She could've —why wasn't she screwing her boyfriend in *his* room? No, of course it was ours. If I had just stayed in the common room, waited it out, we wouldn't be in this mess.

By *we*, I mean me.

I wouldn't be in this mess.

"I'm going to be sick," I announce.

Olivia hops off the bed and grabs her trash can. She pulls out the liner and thrusts it at me. "No puking on my bed."

I take it, gripping the lip hard. "This is going to be the worst thing ever."

She grimaces. "Maybe no one will see it?"

I glare at her. I don't know if he boosted that public post or *what*, but it has more than two thousand likes. *Two thousand people have seen my ass.*

"Maybe no one we know will see it," she amends.

I release the trash can and bury my face in my hands. "Oh, this is the worst thing in the freaking world. Can you just kill me now?"

"I'd be too lonely without you." She puts her arm around my shoulders. "It'll be okay. No matter what happens."

My phone dings with an incoming notification, and I suck in a fast breath. We both go still.

When I don't move, Olivia asks, "Do you want me to...?"

"No." I clear my throat and lift my head. "No, um, I'll do it."

"I'll give you a minute." She slips off the bed and snags her ID, and a second later, the door closes with a click behind her.

Okay.

My hands tremble, but I reach for the phone. Type in my password, then open the app. There's a new post from —from me. From Camden. I take a breath, then another. Just the video—no caption, no tags. Nothing else except for that little lock icon on the top right, indicating it's a private post for subscribers.

I press play.

It's at a different angle than the photo posted before, but I'd guess it was the same night. It's like the whole thing is staged. The bed in the empty room, the swath of light that cuts across my legs.

For a long moment, nothing happens. Then the screen goes fuzzy, like a glitch, and someone—*Camden*—is on top of me.

I'm still asleep.

I didn't wake up.

Horror and, worse, something deeper, floods through me. Something that feels a lot like arousal.

A voice in the back of my head whispers, *Why do you like that?*

Why am I not more pissed he broke into my room and fucked me while I slept?

I watch the whole thing. Never once does the video show either of our faces. He stays above it, never pressing his weight down into my body. He stills, then the video glitches again. It shows me, alone, curling onto my side away from the camera.

The screen goes black.

I shut off my phone and stare at the wall, willing my heart to calm down.

Turned on? Maybe.

But he shared it—he's making money off of this.

Whatever anger I lacked while watching the video compounds as I consider the implications of how I just watched it. I paid four fucking dollars to watch my own sex tape.

That's *my* money.

I'm still stewing when Olivia returns a few minutes later. She peeks in, and when she sees what can only be my rage face, she enters fully. I focus on her and blow out a long, slow breath.

"I'm going to kill him," I say quietly.

Olivia's lips twitch. "Just tell me where to meet you with the shovels."

CAMDEN

I couldn't check my phone on the bus. Royal was sitting right beside me, and I'm not quite sure how I'd explain away the WatchMe app on my phone... logged in under his sister's name.

It screamed trouble, so I avoided it. I shut off my notifications, because I kept getting pings with comments and likes.

Harper is shut away in her room when we get home. Exhausted, we all wordlessly file upstairs and go into our rooms. I, along with the rest of my team, had shed our suit jackets and ties on the bus, replacing the starched dress shirts with t-shirts and hoodies stuffed in our hockey bags.

So it's only my dress slacks and loafers I need to shed, plus the hoodie, to flop into bed.

Once there, buried under the covers, I open the app and scroll the notifications. There are too many, and finally, I just shake my head and switch over to the insights.

Thousands of new subscribers.

Thousands.

The monetary amount makes my jaw drop.

I go to the post and scroll through the comments. Most of them are flattering... and over half are explicit.

What the fuck is wrong with people?

I close out of it and silence the notifications. Fuck that. Fuck Harper for her sex appeal, for sleeping in that position, for not waking up. Even though I really didn't want her to wake up.

Before I fully register my actions, I'm out of bed. Out of my room. Sneaking down the hallway to the last door—*her door.* I reach for the nail, but I test the knob first. Just in case.

It turns easily.

My brows furrow, but I crack the door and peek in. The bed is a mess, but I can't quite make out her form. I enter fully and approach the bed, then let out a huff of irritation.

Empty bed.

"Where did you go?" I ask the air.

It, not surprisingly, doesn't have an answer.

Deterred, at least temporarily, I return to my room. But sleep does not come easily. And when it does, my dreams are plagued with Harper.

HARPER

"Should we take over-under bets on when you'll go back to the hockey house?" Olivia eyes me. "Like, for real. Not just running back to get fresh clothes and go to class."

That's exactly where we're going now.

We decided to walk—it's *only* two miles, Olivia said—and she rationalized we can call a rideshare car to get back after my photography class. The wind is cold, and my face is freezing. We're almost back to Framingham State, luckily. We take side streets that let us avoid the arena, cutting through residential housing.

Eventually, we come up on the hockey house. My brother and Camden both should be on campus at this hour. I don't really give a shit about the other two.

Olivia follows me up the porch steps and inside, and she closes the door fast. Inside is a lot warmer, but it's just a blessing to be out of the wind. I pull my hood down and rub my hands together.

"What do you need for the photography class?"

"Just the camera in my closet and my backpack." I hurry toward the stairs.

Olivia had an early class, and now she's done for the day. *Lucky her.* But she volunteered to set up in the library while I'm at class, then accompany me back to St. James. *If* I'm not ready to just stay here.

Which I'm not.

I'm getting paranoid. I keep thinking someone's watching me. Or, well, more people. Everyone. They're going to take one glance and recognize me from the WatchMe page.

It's dumb, since my face hasn't been in it. It's in the tiny profile picture at the top of the page, though.

And my full name.

I grimace and continue upstairs, bypassing Camden's and Royal's rooms. Then Lucas's and Connor's. All the doors are shut except the bathroom.

At the end of the hall, I pause with my hand on the doorknob. How many times has Camden come looking for me?

Probably not often at all. I wasn't there when he posted it, and then I spent another night at Olivia's. Tonight will be the third.

Perhaps the final?

Depends on how many question mark texts my brother sends.

I step inside and take a breath. A floral scent hits me —it practically smacks me in the face. My muscles all lock, but my heart jumps into overdrive.

I look around the room frantically, but it's empty. Just the air mattress, same as before. The open closet. My gaze swings back to the bed. I left it unmade, but someone clearly took the time to straighten my bedding. It looks... *lumpy?*

My brows furrowed, I approach like something will bite, and fling back the comforter.

Spread across the sheets are a dozen pink roses.

Max.

Or a sick joke by Camden?

I stumble backward, putting distance between me and the roses. My stomach churns, and I swallow hard.

"Olivia!" I shout.

She rushes upstairs and down the hall, skidding to a halt in the open doorway. She gasps, then chokes.

"Please tell me Camden did this," I whisper. "*He* doesn't know where I live—"

"It was absolutely Camden." Olivia steps forward. She's the brave one, going straight up to the bed and picking up one of the flowers. "But..."

Light spots dance in my peripheral vision. "But, what?"

"You probably didn't tell him Max used to cut off the thorns." Olivia holds up one of the long-stemmed roses, her thumb right below where a thorn has been removed.

Fuck.

I back up until I hit the wall and slide down it.

Olivia makes a noise in her throat. "He's just guessing. You haven't been here. So... he can't know. All he knows, probably, is your brother lives here."

"Okay." I squeeze my eyes shut tight for a long moment, trying to regain some control over myself. After a long moment, I look up at her. "You're right."

"Come on." Olivia holds out her hands. "Deep breath."

I let her pull me to my feet. She rummages around on my desk, in the drawers, and pulls out a notebook I'd labeled for my photography class. She tucks it into my backpack and finds my camera. My laptop is already in the bag.

"I'm going to walk you to and from class, and I will punch that asshole in the face if I see him." She holds out my bag. "And then we're going to tell your brother."

I shake my head. "Where will I go if *here* isn't safe? Home? That's not safe either."

She quiets.

Telling my brother...

I march over to my desk and grab the small trash bin, then make quick work sweeping the flowers into it. They barely fit, and my fingers crush some of the petals in my hurry. The pink stains my fingers, my white sheets. It's like the color has bled.

"Can you open the window? Let some air in—"

"On it," Olivia replies.

I carry the flowers out of my room. Straight downstairs, out the front door, and around to the side of the house where the garbage bins live. I dump them all in and slam the lid shut.

If he's watching...

I keep the mask over my features in place and return

inside. Olivia has further removed any trace of the bits of petals left behind, and even the scent is lessening. The chilly breeze sweeps in, lifting strands of my hair.

I swing my bag over my shoulder and motion to her. Clothes can wait—they're the least of my problem now. My skin crawls just standing in this room any longer.

And besides, I'm about to be late for my photography class.

"Leave it," I advise. "Let's get out of here."

My TIME on campus is spent oscillating between trying to focus on class, looking over my shoulder, and checking that damn app. The number of subscribers on my page has only grown, and it makes me sick every time the page refreshes.

But I cannot stop.

I also can't stop scrolling the comments on the video, searching for something to indicate Max Keegan is watching. If he found it.

What if he did? And that's what prompted the roses?

"Ms. Shay?"

I jerk.

My photography professor stands at the front of my row. "You okay?"

I slowly look around the rest of the room, and my body goes hot when it registers there's not a single other person remaining.

"Oh, gosh, I'm sorry, Professor." I scramble to flip my notebook shut and collect the assortment of pens I was using... until, apparently, my mind wandered enough that I missed the end of the lesson. "Don't know where my head went."

She chuckles. "It happens to the best of us. I got a little long-winded at the end anyway. Once students get a glazed look to their eye, I know to wrap it up."

"I really like this class." Everything sufficiently gathered, I swing my bag over my shoulder and pause at the front of the room. "I'm looking forward to trying out the technique we've been going over recently."

While we've barely dug in for the semester, I've been intrigued by the methods Professor Bianca has introduced.

My rented camera was previously stored in my desk drawer in my dorm room. Then wrapped in eighteen layers of clothing. Then, carefully placed in the closet.

Now, it is back in its case in my backpack. We bring them in on Mondays and do a sort of show-and-tell at the beginning of the class. I didn't have much to show, just some landscapes that seemed dull in comparison to the other students' photos.

My professor sees me to the door and pauses. "For this upcoming week... if you don't mind me suggesting this, Harper, perhaps you could return to what you originally said you liked? Portraits, if I'm not mistaken?"

I frown. "I... could."

Olivia has often been my subject, so I could ask her. Speaking of—I spot her through the doorway, leaning against the far wall with her bag at her side.

"Word around campus is you're related to one of our hockey players," Professor Bianca adds. "Not that I get caught up in student gossip, but I've always found a personal touch can help inspiration."

I nod slowly, imagining how asking Royal to pose for me would go. Probably not too well. I suppose I'd have to cave and return to the hockey house for that to happen.

"I'll think on that. Thanks, Professor."

14

CAMDEN

Harper is gone.

We returned home from the hockey game late on Saturday. It was practically Sunday morning, at that point. The video had been posted. But her room, her *bed*, was empty.

Then empty Sunday night, too, with no trace of her throughout the day.

Royal said something about her shopping with Olivia, but that didn't seem to hold water when the sun set, and his sister did not come waltzing in through the front door.

I know because I was hunkered down in the living room, with my gaze on the front windows, for most of the day.

Now it's *Wednesday*, and I'm getting sick of looking in at her empty room. She's been back to her room at least once—on Monday night, I snuck in to find her previously rumpled bed made, neat as a pin—but I haven't run across her.

It's fucking frustrating. I wanted a reaction—I wanted assurance she wouldn't talk to her brother. I wanted to twist the knife a little bit.

And she decides to remove herself from the equation?

My anger builds upon itself. Each time I think about her, each time I check for her, it spikes. The shots of adrenaline have been messing with my sleep. My eyes feel like sandpaper. I was playing catch up from our late Saturday, and I only seem to be getting farther behind.

Why can't she just follow the fucking rules?

I rub my face.

I sit through class, forcing some modicum of will power to pay attention to the professor, and when it ends, I bolt. The Administration building is too warm. Too full of bodies pressing close. I trot down the wide, marble stairs, around and around until I hit the ground floor, and exit onto the quad.

"Hey!" Lucas jogs over. He slaps my hand. "Some guys are gonna go to the pizza place for dinner tonight. You in?"

My attention is dragged across the quad, toward the student center. To the girl walking at an angle away from me. Backpack on, hands in her pockets. Head bent against the relentless wind.

Harper Shay, at long last.

I straighten, glancing from Lucas to her. It's really no contest when I compare the two. Continue with him or go follow her?

I've been waiting for some blowup. Some reaction to the note I left on the mirror.

Nothing.

Did she find the page?

"I gotta run, man," I say to my teammate. "Catch you at dinner."

He nods, and I jog off in Harper's direction. She's just disappearing inside the student center, and it takes me another minute to reach the doors. Ahead is the entrance to the dining hall, but it's closed while they change over from breakfast to lunch.

To my left is a gym and the staircase that goes up to the lounges on the second floor.

Perhaps that's where she went.

I take the stairs two at a time and pause at the top. I give the open area a quick sweep, and just when I'm about to give up, I find her. Rather, the back of her head.

She's tucked in a corner all alone, facing the huge windows that overlook the quad.

Well, she's not alone anymore.

I approach, pausing to look over her shoulder at the textbook open in her lap. A notebook is balanced on her knee, and she's taking notes by hand.

In a world where students highlight right in the book, or take notes in the margins—or, perhaps worse, type everything into their laptops—this seems like an old-school method.

So I do the natural thing and squeeze between her and the next chair, and I snatch the notebook from her leg. Her pen skates across the bottom of the page, a word cut off.

She lets out a squeak, but she's not fast enough to stop

me. I fall into the seat beside her, ignoring her fully while I thumb through the pages.

Lots of notes that don't really make sense.

"What is this?" I glance over to find Harper *glaring* at me.

I smile. I didn't really know what I was going to get from her. Shame or embarrassment, maybe? But anger is a whole lot better. It matches mine.

"Math," she snips at me. "Give it back."

I squint at the page and keep my façade. "There are no numbers."

"I know." She reaches for it. "It's theoretical."

I keep it away, leaning back in my chair. "Theoretical math? You're a freshman, aren't you? This seems like a high-level course for someone in their first semester."

Strands of hair fall in her face. They flutter with her huff, and she's practically hanging off her chair to swat at the notebook. I catch her hand and tug a bit more.

Her index finger has a little stain of pink on it. She smells good—floral. I haven't noticed that scent on her before. Perhaps it's a new perfume? Borrowed from whoever she's crashing with?

Her legs leave the floor, and she squeaks.

"Hmm." I run my finger along the inside of her wrist. "Feisty little thing, aren't you?"

She yanks.

I hold fast.

Her cheeks flush, and she meets my gaze. "I'm going to make your life a living hell."

"Ah." I tap her palm. "But how will you do that if I

can do the same to you? One click, and that video goes public."

"You've already used my real name. People can find me. Is that what you want? Especially after you heard about Max, huh? You thought, gee, she has a stalker, let's make it super easy for him to find a video of her *having sex*." She scowls. "If you can even call it that."

She's cute when she's mad. She's wearing an over-sized sweater, but at *this* angle, I have a view down the gaping collar to the black bralette that cups her tits.

Oh, to be the lace pressed against her nipples.

I drop the notebook on top of her bag, then rise. Still holding her wrist, I hoist her to her feet. One quick pull, and she collides with my chest.

She's hottest when she's off-balance. When I can feel her shape against my body.

When she doesn't know what's coming next.

"How about... you sneak into *my* room tonight?" I suggest. "You blow me to my satisfaction, and I'll change the name on the WatchMe profile."

She blinks fast. Thinking it over? Trying to hide the shot of lust that probably went straight between her legs?

I tip my head. "That would require you returning to the hockey house, of course."

"Of course," she echoes. "You want me to suck your dick, and you'll change the name on the account to what?"

"Hmm." I tilt my head. "Your porn star name could be something sweet. Candy, maybe. No, not with that expression. Sour Patch Kid is a mouthful and might send the wrong message. I don't know, Harper. I'll think on it."

I release her, and she stumbles back.

I don't move while she gathers her notebook, textbook, bag. She doesn't bother shoving everything into it, just clutches it all to her chest and speeds away.

Well, *I* thought it was a good offer.

Maybe I should call her Venom. She has enough of it inside her. And it's fitting for this school... Harper truly is an FSU Viper.

15

———

HARPER

My mind filters through *the worst that could happen* on my way to the library. Olivia's in class over at her school, but she promised she'd return to meet me here later. The FSU library is generally a pretty safe place to be. It's full of other students and staff, at least until dinnertime.

But I wasn't expecting Camden to intercept me—or his proposition. Changing the name on the account wouldn't solve everything, but it would help. It could stop Max from finding the page—and right now, Max is my biggest problem.

Which means giving in to his demand.

Great.

I pull out my phone and scroll through my recent messages. Olivia checking in, Royal...

ROYAL

> Seriously, you can't stay at Olivia's
> forever

> Blink twice if you're alive

> Well, Connor said he heard you and
> Olivia in the house the other day, so nice
> to know you're still breathing

> Your stuff got delivered

> Me and Lucas built it this afternoon, so
> it's all set for you to come back

> ...

> Are you pissed at me or something?

> Don't make me resort to calling Mom...

Those were sent over the last three days. Guilt hits me.

I send him back a thumbs-up emoji, which isn't a lot but it does prove I'm breathing, and switch to Olivia's thread.

ME

> I think I need to go back to the hockey
> house tonight

Her reply comes immediately.

OLIVIA

> With a knife under your pillow just in
> case, right???

I snicker, but it dies off relatively fast. Suddenly, the idea of Camden sneaking in and repeating what he did before is the least of my worries. I already know my objective: go to *him*. Get the profile name changed.

Watch out for stalkers hiding in my closet.

"Hey! Harper!"

I tuck my phone in my pocket and turn.

Cynthia hurries across the lawn toward me. She's dressed for winter, with a thick scarf wrapped around her neck, and a puffy coat zipped up to it. All that's missing is the hat with a pom-pom and knit mittens.

"I've been searching for you everywhere." She joins me on the path and loops her arm through mine. "Gosh. You were a good roommate, you know? But now that you've moved out, they replaced you with some nerd who gets up at the crack of dawn. And she chews so much gum—but I'm pretty sure she swallows it when she's done. You're supposed to spit out gum, Harper, it can stay in your stomach for *seven years*."

Wow.

I try to untangle myself, but she only holds harder.

"So she leaves to go to the gym, and I get a knock on the door. Open it up, and it's this hottie looking for *you*."

I freeze. My mind immediately goes to Max Keegan. "Excuse me?"

"Some hockey guy. But if it's not Camden Church, I don't know his name." She lifts a shoulder. "I've seen him around before, though."

"So not some random weirdo?"

She shakes her head. "Nah. Definitely a teammate."

I blow out a long breath.

"Probably Royal," I guess. "My brother. I haven't been in contact in the past few days, so... he probably didn't know where else to go."

"Right. Well, he assumed you were with me, which is really sweet but also kind of misguided. I had to inform him that since you moved out, the housing department assigned me a hippie nut." Her voice drops. "I can't even have sex with my boyfriend, Harper. She doesn't *care*. We were getting frisky under the covers one night and all I could hear was her gum snapping."

I wrinkle my nose. That sounds like the definition of a buzzkill, it's true. But also, this just proves moving out of that room was the right call for me. This new roommate sounds like the perfect match for Cynthia and her inconsiderate antics.

"Don't worry about my brother," I say. "I'm going to his house tonight."

She nods along. "Right, well, that doesn't solve—"

"I'm sorry, Cynthia, I'm late to my next class." I succeed in freeing my arm and make a sharp right. I veer away from her. "Good to see you, though! Thanks for letting me know about Royal."

She calls something else, but I ignore her and duck through the science building. I emerge on the other side alone and slow my pace for the walk back to the hockey house.

It's funny—I know Royal had been texting me, but I didn't think he was actually worried about not seeing me. Knowing he even checked my dorm brings a newfound warmth to my chest.

He cares.

I know he does, of course. It's that I'm-the-only-one-allowed-to-bully-you vibe. He also can be nice some-times. But... I don't know. I guess while we're *close*, we're not share-every-secret close. Or know-where-the-other-is-at-every-second-of-every-day close.

Maybe the appearance of Max has him rattled, even if he doesn't know the half of it.

I glance around on reflex, checking for signs of my stalker. No hair raises on the back of my neck, my ears aren't burning. If he's watching, he's being so subtle my instincts can't detect it.

Perhaps he lost interest.

Either way, I'm not about to stick around and find out.

I make it back to the hockey house unscathed. The front door is unlocked, which is good. I don't think Royal ever gave me a house key. Do they ever lock it?

Guys probably aren't worried about security like me. And if Royal knew the unlocked door only made it easier for Max to sneak in and cover my air mattress in roses... That really just confirms I should tell him. So he can *do* something about it.

Because Camden is right. *Ugh, did you really just think that?* No, no, he is right. I can't stay in hiding forever. And he just offered the perfect carrot dangling out in front of me to bring me back.

The house feels the same as it did the other day. Which is to say: surprisingly normal.

Lucas and Connor, the two other housemates, are on the couch playing a video game. I wave to them on my way by and go straight upstairs.

Royal's door is open.

I knock on the frame and peek in, then enter fully when I spot him at his desk.

His headphones are on, and he doesn't react to my entrance. I really shouldn't do what I'm about to do, but the closer I get, the more I can hear the tinny music blasting in his ears. And it just seems like a perfect opportunity.

I creep forward, then pounce and grab his shoulders. I yell, for good measure.

He shouts. His whole body jerks, nearly flinging me away, but his wide-eyed expression of fear catapults me into hysterics. He catches a glimpse of me and swears, knocking his headphones off.

"What the fuck, Harper?"

His expression—horror, then anger—is perfect.

Priceless.

I'm too busy dying of laughter to answer him.

He grips me around the waist and picks me up off my feet. I screech, still laughing, as he throws me over his shoulder and stalks out of the room.

"Put me down!" I kick.

"You're gonna pay for that," he warns.

Uh-oh.

"And for not responding to my texts for two days."

Right.

He heads away from the stairs—I suppose it's good he's not planning on tossing me in a pile of leaves in the backyard or something—and opens a door. I lift my head enough to see the dresser he built against one wall. My suitcases all neatly arranged by the closet. New hangers.

He tips forward, and I yelp again when I fall backward. I hit a mattress, and my brows furrow. This isn't the squishy, unbalanced air mattress.

There's a headboard.

"It's—"

"Yeah," he mutters, glancing around. "Your room. A real bed. New sheets and comforter, curtesy of Mom. It's been waiting for you, but you decided to have an extended sleepover with Olivia."

A lump forms in my throat.

"Mom wants a call back," he adds.

"Tell me you didn't mention—"

"Your stalker?" Royal plants his hands on his hips and stares me down. "No. But you should."

I should tell you, too.

The good news? The room doesn't smell like roses anymore.

It takes me a second to fully take in the room. It actually does feel like... well, like *mine*. This seems to be an invitation to stay. Even if Max never shows his face on the FSU campus again. Even if the flowers were a sick joke by Camden and not *him*.

"Thank you," I whisper. "This was a lot."

"Damn straight." He offers his hand, and I let him help me to my feet. He wraps his arm around me. It's easy to rest my cheek on his chest and forget about the rest of it.

Namely, *Camden.*

The menace down the hall.

16

HARPER

This is insane.

We're having a roommates' dinner this evening. The five of us sit around their kitchen table, eating a meal that Lucas and Connor prepared. Because apparently this is their *thing*. Once a week, usually on a Wednesday, two of the four—now five—make dinner for everyone.

They went with a cheesy chicken-broccoli-rice casserole, garlic bread, and a salad.

I'm not complaining. I'm just confused.

"Is it always you two and then Royal and Camden?" I ask Lucas.

He seems the friendliest, beyond my brother. But his mouth is currently stuffed with garlic bread, and I've seen him talk with a full mouth too many times to count.

"We usually draw cards at the beginning of the month," Connor supplies. He glances at Royal. "We're gonna have to revise that a bit if you're staying, little Lawson."

I frown. "It's Shay."

"Right."

"Harper can go with Church next week," Lucas says.

I stiffen. So much for him being the friendly one.

Royal rolls his eyes. "You guys hate my cooking that much?"

"You just have a tendency to burn shit, man." Connor eyes me. "You didn't inherit that same gene, did you, baby Lawson?"

For fuck's sake.

"No," I say through my teeth. "I'm a fine cook."

I can't even look in Camden's direction. He said nothing about my return this afternoon. He's said nothing at all, really, since he arrived just in time for this meal. But I think if I looked at him, he'd smirk, and I'd lose it.

Emotionally.

Because I'm *insane* for coming back here on the heels of his proposition.

"So is Church." Lucas grins. "So it's settled. Royal can be with me or Connor the following week, and we'll put him in charge of salads or some shit."

"Why doesn't Church just do the same?" I point my fork at Camden, still focusing on Lucas. "Unless you like bad meals."

Camden scoffs. "I try to tell Royal what to do and I come out of that kitchen bruised."

Royal rolls his eyes. "Hardly."

"Wooden spoons are no joke."

I have a sharp memory of being smacked in the thigh with a wooden spoon, wielded by my brother when we were kids. It absolutely left bruises. I find myself smiling —then quickly try to put a leash on it.

No smiling at the jerk who's posting sex videos of you for profit.

My gaze flicks to the jerk unwillingly. He looks too perfect. The messed-up hair that could've been crafted by a magazine stylist, his blue eyes, the cords of his neck. Then, of course, the picture of his naked ass cheeks flexing as he fucked that girl the first night, comes unbidden to the forefront of my mind.

Heat crawls up my cheeks. I really shouldn't be thinking about him naked at a time like this.

Back to the matter at hand. "How about I take Royal, and Church can..." *fuck off?*

Camden rests his elbow on the table and braces his chin on his fist. He meets my gaze, his brows lifting. There's that smirk. "You're not a team player, baby Lawson?"

Royal snickers. I clench my jaw.

"If you're half decent, then you and Church would make a decent meal. Please only let us suffer once." That from Connor.

Ugh.

"I think it's a solid plan," Royal says. "In fact, maybe Harper could just take my place every week. Since you're not paying rent."

My jaw drops. "I will pay—"

"You have literally no money," he interrupts. "Food is more than fair. Better than asking you to clean the bathroom."

I wrinkle my nose at that thought. Did it cross my

mind? Yes. What is it with guys and not brushing their beard hair out of the freaking sink? But then, miraculously, it'll be clean. Same with the kitchen. One day there will be dishes stacked in the sink, and the next, nothing. So I guess that's one chore that the guys share.

"Fine." I tap my index finger on the table and glare at my brother. "But—"

"You're not happy about it, yeah, yeah." He takes a bite. "What else is new?"

BAD IDEA. Bad, bad, bad idea.

And yet.

The house has been quiet for a while. The hour is late. I ease my bedroom door open and pause, peeking out down the hall. There's a night light plugged into an outlet near the bathroom, but other than that—dark and empty.

Everyone has gone to bed, and I am about to do something insane.

Like follow a demand from Camden Church.

I move down the hall, my footsteps nearly silent, and stop in front of his door. My heart suddenly speeds up. I could go back to bed—it's not too late for that. I could live with my name being on that WatchMe account.

But... no, I can't.

I take a deep breath and put my fingers on his doorknob. A test. Then, carefully, fully palm it and twist.

It opens easily on silent hinges.

The room is dark, but not *dark*-dark. The blinds are

open, letting in the glow from the streetlights outside. There's some night-light-looking thing on his desk, a ball of glowing yellow that just barely beats back the shadows around it.

And there's Camden, sitting on his bed. His feet are on the floor, his hands resting on his knees.

He doesn't say anything when I enter. No quips, no rude remarks.

I close the door behind me and lock it, and I steel myself for what I have to do. If he doesn't make it easy on me...

He won't, a small voice in the back of my head whispers.

It's only when I get closer can I see his eyes. The way they linger on my face for a moment before trailing down my body.

I didn't know what to wear, so I just... I'm in a t-shirt and shorts. Nothing crazy, sure, but a little alluring. What if I came in here and he didn't get hard at the thought of a blow job? I've heard of girls putting it flaccid in their mouth, and while that's fine... I don't really want to have to convince him to get there for me.

Maybe I'm crazy.

I'm definitely crazy.

He's still not saying anything, so I match his energy. I step between his legs and stare down at him for a long moment. His head is level with my breasts. His hair is messed up, either from sleep or dragging his fingers through it. He's bare-chested. His abdomen flexes, the ridiculous six-pack evident.

When I go to my knees, he sucks in the quietest

breath. I keep eye contact for a moment longer, then drop my gaze to his lap.

There's a tent in his boxers.

I inch forward, closer, and lift the elastic waistband. I pull it down, exposing his length. I run my tongue along my upper lip. My nerves buzz, but he hasn't so much as shifted an inch. Just his eyes, his gaze hot on my face. They stay with me when I lean down and take him in my mouth.

When he doesn't cup the back of my head or dictate my movements, I swirl my tongue and rise until just the tip remains. I go down again, deeper, and hollow my cheeks when he hits the back of my throat.

He lets out a low groan.

I hunt for those sounds as I continue, desperate to drive him crazy simply because I can. A thrill comes over me, a rush I can't ignore. *Don't want to ignore.* Instead, I lean into it until he can't resist, and his fingers slip through my hair. His nails scratch my scalp, but the pressure doesn't change.

Not until he sucks in a breath, and he pushes down.

I'm already down, but I suck hard anyway. He comes in my mouth. I swallow around him, my throat working, until there's nothing else. His hand disappears.

I straighten and wipe my mouth with the back of my hand, but I can't seem to meet his gaze.

Camden catches my wrist. He tows me closer, so I automatically rise on my knees.

His other hand drifts to my face. My chin. He presses down, opening my mouth, and runs his finger along my lower lip.

Then he releases me.

I stand up and step back. The last thing I need—or want—is to be seen fixing myself up after *that*. I'm not embarrassed. I came in here with a purpose.

"The name." My voice rasps out.

"Already changed."

I stiffen.

His low chuckle fills the room. "Go scuttle back to your room and check if you don't believe me."

I... I'm going to do just that. I avoid his gaze, and something on his desk catches my attention.

A single, crushed rose.

Pink, if I had to guess.

My stomach somersaults, and humiliation burns through me. It's hot and quick, sealing my mortification. It *was* him. He took what I admitted to my brother, what we explained about the stalker, and used it to spike fear through me.

All without seeing my reaction.

Is that why he pulled that from the outside bin? Just to get another taste of my terror?

Well, he's not going to get it now.

I pivot and flee, and I don't stop until I'm back in the safety of my room. I grab my phone, charging on the new nightstand Royal got me, and open the WatchMe app.

Sure enough, the sole account I follow has changed its name. I'm not sure what I was expecting, but my stomach swoops at the sight.

The Voyeur.

CAMDEN

Editing the footage of the blow job takes time. It also makes me relive it, and before long, I'm hard again. I rewatch it once through, then post it. It's been over an hour—what are the odds Harper went to bed?

Guess I'm about to find out.

My gaze flicks to the rose on my desk. I had grabbed it out to ask her about it, but she only cast a fleeting glance and then rushed away. Maybe the roses came from Connor or Lucas. Or Royal. It wouldn't be the first time a girl has given a guy flowers. Sure, it's a bit odd... The trash already went out, though, and I'd feel a little more like a creep if I questioned the guys.

Something about roses tickles at my memory, but I can't remember the significance.

I sneak into the hall and creep down toward Harper's room. I imagine she checked her phone for the name on the account. As promised, I erased all signs of her real name, replacing it with little things to needle her. Calling her a voyeur was just the icing on the cake. There are references to peeking into her world. In this scenario, *she's* not the voyeur—her followers are.

And maybe I am, too.

Did she understand?

Her door is unlocked—another sign I take with a smile.

Is she asleep? Or perhaps she's waiting for me?

I slip into her darkened room and pause, my back to the closed door. I was around while Royal and Lucas assembled the furniture and hefted the mattress up the staircase, but I didn't offer to help. Even if I'm all for Harper being within easy reach, I didn't want to give Royal any ideas about my enthusiasm.

Maybe enthusiasm is the wrong word.

I'm just... horny.

Obsessed.

Her deep breathing fills the room, and I latch on to that noise. She must've already been tossing and turning, because she's flat on her stomach, one leg hiked up and exposed. The blankets are rumpled, barely covering her.

And, oh, she's naked.

Naughty Harper.

I set up my phone to record, taking a moment to check the angle and lighting. It'll do. I shed my clothes off-camera and approach her. My movements are slow and steady. Peel down the blankets. Expose her body.

Anticipation thrums through me. It's been too long. Days. *Eons.*

Same thing, really.

I don't bother trying to adjust her body—she's fine the way she is. In the perfect position for me to lift her hips up and slide into her. She's soaked, her cunt practically dripping. From touching herself after—*or before*—the blow job, or just from the act of it? I wish I knew.

The not knowing is just as sweet.

I line up, press forward, and somehow withhold the deep groan building in my throat. She feels so fucking good, I don't know how this could be any better.

Maybe if she was awake?

No.

I don't think she quite deserves that yet. Not when any day, she could reveal the secrets between us to her brother. I don't doubt the lengths he would go to spite me for touching her.

When I'm buried fully inside her, I slowly lower myself down. My front presses to her back, and I slide my hands under her. I cup her tits, pinch at her nipples. My mouth lands at the crook of her neck, where it slopes into her shoulder, and I inhale her sweet scent.

Not floral, but more like honey.

It makes me want to take a taste.

My hips move, the squeeze of her cunt around my shaft making staying still nearly unbearable. Out, and sharp back in. My stamina should be better now that she took the edge off with her mouth. And feeling the soft planes of her body under mine just makes every sensation better.

She shifts, a low groan escaping her.

I fuck her harder. Our bodies jerk with every thrust, until I sense her waking up. Her breath comes quicker, and she tries to roll—only to be held immobile.

She struggles. Her head snaps back, and only a quick

twist to the side keeps my nose safe. Her panic comes back double when that little move doesn't work, and it feels different than the other times we've been together.

I pull out and grasp at her flailing arms, manhandling her until she's on her back. Her chest heaves, and I pin her wrists over her head. Stretched out over her, my head even with hers.

"It's me."

Her eyes flutter, the glazed panic finally receding when her gaze latches on to my face.

"Camden?"

I scowl. "Who else sneaks into your bed at night?"

Her mouth opens and closes.

I narrow my eyes, but she only shakes her head.

An unfounded fear? Doubtful.

I sigh at the lie of omission. Someone else coming into her bed like this, but causing her irrational fear?

My rage comes out of nowhere.

It's not directed at her, but she's my only target. For what? For not being truthful?

"Just me," I assure her.

I slide my hands down her wrists, over her forearms, her biceps, until I have her throat. Her heartbeat pulses at my fingertips, way too fast to be normal.

"Just me," I repeat as I tighten my grip.

Her hands come to *my* wrists, but she's no match. I put her back to sleep—this time, well, it's a bit forced. She goes slack, and I relax my grip. I spread her legs and push back into her. I take what I need, and when she tenses up, her awareness crawling back, I make sure she stays unconscious. I want her to ride the edge.

In both the sense of being awake and also orgasming.

Like this, looking at the way her breasts sway, and how her throat looks with my hand wrapped around it, my climax approaches faster than I anticipated. My balls tighten, and I spill inside her. I keep moving my hips, fucking her through it, and the tingling sensation feels like heaven and agony.

Finally, I pull out. I run my finger up her center, collecting my cum, and smear it across her lips.

Then, before she can wake, I put my clothes back on, end the recording, and get the fuck out of her room.

I make it almost all the way back to my room. But I glance over my shoulder at her door and crash into a body. Hands grasp my shoulders, shoving me back, and I focus on who's in front of me.

"Dude," Royal grunts. "Watch where you're going."

My body flushes, and I swear, he's one second away from reading the guilt all over my face. And that will be the end of it. Our friendship, my good name on the team —everything.

But instead, he just moves past me, into the bathroom, and closes the door between us.

Safe for another day.

But it doesn't make me feel any better... even if Harper is the last thing on my mind when I finally do close my eyes.

18

HARPER

I wake with a sharp gasp, bolting upright. I search my dark room, the shadows seeming to hold too many monsters to count, and fumble for the lamp on my nightstand. It clicks on, and my eyes burn in the sudden brightness.

Nothing.

Empty room.

Just a sore, aching pussy, a salt-and-musk taste on my lips, and the memory of Camden wrapping his hands around my throat as he fucked me.

I was *sleeping*.

The fear I woke up with—that it was Max hovering above me—melts into rage. I swing the blankets back and stand. I fell asleep naked, but now I jerk on a t-shirt and shorts. I check my phone for the time and freeze at the new notification from WatchMe. Another video posted... and judging by the caption, I'd have to guess it's the blow job.

Asshole.

I take a breath. Pause. I consider what to do, how to pay him back for this, and grab my phone. Plus something else, hidden deep in my nightstand. Supplies in hand, I stalk out of the room.

The hallway is empty. The house dark and silent.

It's perfect, unfortunately, for some stalker to creep in and wreak havoc. Who even knows if the doors downstairs are locked?

I shake my head and rest my fingertips on Camden's doorknob. I don't know if he's expecting me... I don't know how much time has passed since he was in my room, or if he went right to sleep, or if I'm about to walk in on him doing something else.

Is this how he feels when he comes into my room?

Anticipation sings along with my anger, and it pushes me forward. To turn the knob, to slip into his room before one of the other guys ruins the moment and comes out to pee or something.

His room is darker than mine. It takes a long moment for my eyes to adjust, and I strain my ears to catch any sound.

His breathing.

It's steady, slow, and deep. He's sleeping.

I grit my teeth and tap the screen of my phone, using that tiny bit of light to guide my steps to the edge of his bed. He's splayed out on his back, one arm over his head. The other is on his stomach.

He doesn't look cruel like this.

He just looks...

Harper Shay, do not say handsome.

I glance around, and my gaze lands on his hockey bag. I leave his side and crouch before it, carefully unzipping it and fishing around. When my fingers find the familiar texture of tape, I smile. It's not duct tape, but it'll do.

Ten painstaking minutes later, Camden's arms are secured over his head. His wrists have been thoroughly taped to his headboard.

The laces from his skates probably would've been better, but they're not in his bag for some reason.

Whatever.

I also opened the blinds on his two wide windows, letting in a bit of light. Enough to see without squinting anyway.

I bite my lip. He either didn't wake up—I made sure to go *so* slow—or he's the world's best actor. I glance to where I set my phone after I found the tape. It's been recording this whole time, but I'm not sure I want to... Yeah, fuck it.

No one has to see it if it comes out like shit.

I slide his blankets off his body, kick off my sleep shorts and straddle his hips. I let my weight settle on him, and only then do I let myself register the sharp burn of arousal between my legs. I knew it was there. I woke up with the sensation, woke up *knowing* what happened.

And now I'm going to take what I need from him.

I reach down and palm his dick. I take a second to work my fingers through the gap in his boxers and grip him directly, slowly stroking him to hardness. When he's tented up, I shift forward. He doesn't react when I expose his length and navigate it to my slit. I'm wet from his edging *and* his cum, and it makes accepting his size all the easier.

My breath comes out in a short exhale when he fills me.

On top… it's a different angle like this. I roll my hips, taking him deeper, and my eyes flutter.

No. I need to focus.

I push his shirt up, exposing his abdomen, his stomach, his chest.

He has a six-pack while sleeping. I didn't really know that was a thing, unless he's flexing. My gaze whips to his face, but his eyes are still shut.

Maybe he should join me in consciousness.

I lean forward, putting my face over his. With one hand, I cover his mouth.

With the other, I pinch his nose.

Wait for it.

The deprivation of air snaps him awake. He jerks under me, every muscle in his body cording.

"Shh," I say in some mockery of what he said to me, "it's just me."

He thrashes, and I release his nose. His nostrils flare when he inhales. His gaze cuts through me, so different from his sleeping, peaceful expression. His biceps leap as he yanks at his wrists, and his brows furrow when they don't move.

I used a lot of tape.

His nostrils flare again, and his jaw works under my

fingers. My palm is clapped to his lips, my nails digging into his cheek.

But his fury is nothing compared to the shock that flickers across his face when I roll my hips.

"Oh," I groan. I lift up a little and lower back down, and he hits a deep part inside me that needs it again. "You feel good like this."

He shakes his head, glaring.

"No, no." I move again, rolling. The micromovement sends shivers of pleasure through me. "You don't need this—*I* do."

He says something. The words get caught, muffled against my palm, and I don't really give a shit what he wanted me to know. It could've been a swear, for all I know.

That would ruin the vibe.

Speaking of vibe...

I lean over and snatch the bullet vibrator from his nightstand. It springs to life in my fingers, and I put it on my clit.

I groan louder. My hips jerk at the sensation.

Knowing I could've done this on my own, in my room, in peace, filters through my mind. And maybe Camden's, too. But it's all the better to torture him while I'm at it.

So he just watches, bound, while I take my pleasure from his cock—which only seems to grow harder inside me, pulsing every time he bottoms out inside me—and the vibrator.

As worked up as I was, it barely takes any time at all before my orgasm shudders through my body. My pussy squeezes, my back arches. He shakes his head again, and my hand slips off his mouth.

"Jesus, Harper," he breathes. His hips jerk, thrusting deeper inside me. He fucks me from below while I can't seem to move, my body caught in spiraling pleasure that goes on and on. "What are you doing?"

He doesn't seem pissed—and, surprisingly, my anger has slipped away, as well.

"You don't seem to know how to pleasure a woman properly." I lean away and flash the now-still vibrator in front of his face. "Figured you needed a lesson."

He grunts. His arms yank, muscles cording, but the tape holds fast.

Which is probably for the best.

"You think I needed a *lesson* in how to make you come?" His voice rips out in a low growl.

I narrow my eyes.

"Any woman?" he adds.

I shrug. He flexes, and a new tingling pulse shoots through me.

"How insulting."

"Experience speaks for itself," I murmur.

He rolls his eyes. "I don't need a lesson. And I can prove it."

I snort. "Pass."

"Sit on my face."

I go still.

Of all the things I expected him to say, that was *not* it.

His gaze bores into mine. "Climb up here, hold on to the headboard, and ride my face. Unless you're fucking scared."

That might be one word for it. And yet, I find myself rising up and letting his cock slide out of me, and I crawl forward. I navigate around his tied limbs until his wrists sit on my thighs, and his face is right under me.

All I need to do is lower myself down...

"I'm suddenly worried about suffocating you."

"That should be the least of your concerns." He presses down with his forearms, and I... sit.

His mouth connects with my pussy, and I swear I immediately see stars. I grab on to the headboard, digging my nails into the metal, while he works magic.

I take back what I said—he knows how.

He's just an even bigger asshole for withholding.

His tongue spears me, and I cry out. I slap my hand over my mouth to muffle the sound and grind myself down on him.

More. I need more.

And, like he can hear me, he gives it. He tilts, his tongue flat against my clit, his breath hums out, the slight vibration of it nothing compared to the bullet that made me climax earlier.

Never mind that he breaks into my room and fucks me while I sleep.

Never mind that he films and posts it.

Never mind the rose that was on his desk.

I groan through my teeth, and his low chuckle rumbles up through me.

"Less laughing, more—oh, fuck."

His teeth scrape my clit, and my eyes roll back. He sucks it into his mouth hard, the tip of his tongue flicking against it. Too soon, he goes back down and thrusts inside me. His nose brushes my wetness. I reach down and rub my clit until a spike of pain in my thigh stops me.

He pinched me.

"You're the biggest—" The words die in my throat.

Calling him the *biggest* anything would probably only boost his ego anyway.

My clit is back in his mouth, and the sucking pressure too great. My body tenses, my thighs quiver, and I rise up off him instinctively. His forearms catch my thighs, his elbows digging into my hips. He yanks me back down, and I explode. My pussy clenches on nothing, not for the first time, but he doesn't let up. He keeps sucking, teasing, licking, until sweat collects on the back of my neck, and my thighs shake.

He doesn't care.

My mind blanks when he draws another climax from me.

I tumble sideways off him, collapsing to the bed for only a moment before rolling out of his reach.

Just in case.

I heave a breath once I stand. I pull on my shorts, undoubtedly giving him a nice view of my ass, and retrieve my phone. I end the recording, then glance back over my shoulder at him.

He licks his lips, then grins. "Satisfied? Cut me loose, Harper."

My attention shifts to his erect dick. Worst-case scenario? He traps me in here and puts that to use... which would be fine if I didn't have to be up for class in a few hours. After *three* orgasms, my legs feel a little like jelly.

Besides, he got a blow job *and* sex.

It's only fair if I leave him here.

In fact, that seems like excellent revenge.

"I'm sure with your *proven* oral skills, you can figure out a way to get free on your own." I blow him a kiss, phone in hand. "Sweet dreams, Church."

19

HARPER

CYNTHIA

Your brother is asking if you can meet him at the arena

His phone died? idk. I ran into him on the quad and he recognized me. [blushing emoji] Didn't you mention I have a bf?

Uh, no, you didn't come up. Are you still with him? I'll head there when this class ends.

kk!

I shake off my frown. She's nice enough, but we never got along. She's texted me—and sought me out—more now than when we lived together. I skipped out before Royal or any of the other guys were awake this morning, my stomach in knots.

Something about Camden...

I don't know.

Maybe it was what happened yesterday. The sequence of events that still makes me want to squirm in my seat.

What the hell was I thinking?

It's bad enough that I've indulged in Camden's twisted fantasies—and, maybe, even enjoyed some of them. But I've let him get away with a lot of other shit, too. Like filming me. Posting it to that account. And, most importantly, somehow hiding that all from my brother.

My mind goes back to the rose on his desk. It had looked like he pulled it from the garbage bin outside, but why? He hadn't asked me about it. Didn't use it to torment me. I didn't find the petals scattered across my bed or anything creepy, which is what I would've come to expect.

Ugh.

It might just be a mystery that will never be solved.

I focus back on the professor's lecture and scribble notes to punctuate their key points. Basically, desperately trying not to lose my academic cool in the first semester at FSU... I can't flunk out. Not when Royal somehow maintains a three-point-two grade point average *and* plays hockey.

He would never let me live it down.

And if he finds out what I'm doing with Camden—

Wait. When did it become *with* Camden? And not what Camden is doing *to* me?

Shit, this is worse than I thought. Three orgasms in a row clearly went to my head, impacted my sleep, and made me delusional.

Once class is over, I pack my bag and shoot Royal a text.

> Class just ended, so I'm heading to the arena
>
> Just in case you get your phone charged before I get there

There's no reply, which makes sense. I don't know what he needs from me at the arena. There was one time he forgot his stick at home, and Mom and I had to rush back home to get it.

To be fair, he was ten when that happened, and his teammates ridiculed him so badly, I doubt he's ever forgotten his stick again.

Or helmet.

Or skates.

So... what does that leave?

Oh, God.

The blood drains from my face. I tried to be quiet last night, but what if he *heard*? What if he's packed my shit and decided I'd actually be safer somewhere far, far away from Camden Church?

It wouldn't be the worst idea, but it would also suck now that I've discovered the magic of his mouth. And that's dependent on if he would use it again.

Now, fully convinced Royal is staging an intervention where he feels most comfortable—the arena, obviously—I shrug on my jacket and make the trek down the street from campus.

We're having an unusual cold snap for autumn, and I

hunker down against the sharp wind. The weather doesn't help my darkening mood. There are a million counterarguments coming to mind to convince Royal that what Camden and I are doing is *fine*. Besides the bullying.

But finally, the arena comes into sight, and I head for the players' entrance.

I haul open the door and step inside. I let out a breath, the warmth—and that's saying something—basking my face. But where to find my brother?

They don't practice until this evening, so... locker room?

My stomach twists, and I glance over my shoulder, like Camden Church would be waiting in the shadows to blame me for this.

Great.

I pause at the entrance to the locker room, my weight shifting back and forth.

Going inside seems a bit presumptuous, right?

Eh. A quick phone check reveals absolutely zero messages, and no one responds when I *knock*. Because who knocks on a locker room door?

So... in I go.

"Royal?" I call out.

I haven't been in here before, but there's a long entryway with cabinets, then it opens into the large room. It has cubbies all around the perimeter, the players' names in plaques on the wood. Their gear is all set up, the practice jerseys and helmets, stick tape and random shit. FSU-branded towels.

Everything is in the school colors, purple and white.

It's not super overwhelming. The purple isn't in-your-face loud. I find Royal's cubby, *R. Lawson* on the plaque. And right beside his is *C. Church*.

Typical.

Together always.

I can very clearly remember when Royal found it hard to make friends. When he was always chasing after the team, trying to force himself in where he didn't *quite* fit.

It seems easier with Camden. And maybe Lucas and Connor, too.

Camden doesn't have a ton of stuff in his locker, but his skates catch my attention. It explains why they were missing from his bag last night. The blades might've needed sharpening or replacing.

There's not much else in his cubby. What I *do* know is, Royal probably has candy stashed somewhere in his. Or those electrolyte gels—no, no, they're more likely to be found in his hockey bag, which he'll carry in himself.

Whenever he gets here.

Shit, I didn't think I'd beat him. I check my phone and double-frown as the low-battery alert pops up. Did I forget to plug it in last night after filming?

My cheeks heat.

That's the *last* thing I should be thinking about when Royal is about to stage an intervention.

Late as always, Royal enters the locker room. The hinges squeal upon opening, and there's a *whoosh* as the door swings shut.

I sidestep so it's not super fucking apparent that I was

analyzing Camden's space, instead studiously fixating on Royal's stuff. Specifically, his purple helmet.

"There you are."

My shoulders hike, and I whirl around.

Not my brother.

Max. He strides toward me, his expression neutral. Not happy. Not angry.

I stand up straighter.

He's not wearing Shadow Valley U red today. He wears a purple FSU cap, a black FSU hockey sweatshirt with purple lettering, jeans, and white sneakers. He tilts his head, his eyes steady on me. His blond hair is hidden, but there's no hiding the cool way he regards me with those dark eyes of his.

He's here.

He left the flowers, then?

Not Camden. I never even brought it up with him—just saw the flower on his desk and assumed it was all part of the torture. I refused to mention it, in fact.

But what if I had?

What if I told Royal the truth?

I bite back a scoff. This situation would've still happened, just as Max designed. He found a way to get me alone.

Who knows how long he's been watching?

"Harper, darling. I think you've been avoiding me." He pauses in the middle of the room, dropping a large duffel bag at his side. It hits the floor with a dull *thud.*

I open and close my mouth, but the words seem to get stuck. I swallow against my sudden fear, my gaze glued to the bag. What's in it? Things to murder me? Or kidnap me? My mind goes to ropes, blindfolds, handcuffs. A knife or gun. Something to subdue me if I don't cooperate with his fantasy.

His expression suddenly clears.

"It's my fault, isn't it? I told you how I felt, but I didn't follow through enough." He nods, more to himself than me. "I understand that, Harper, I do. My mother was always waiting on my father. He told her so many lies that she just *believed*. It's better this way. It's better I prove myself. The roses were a weak attempt."

I shake my head. I used to read about stalkers. The kind that turned violent—*just in case*. That's what I told myself. What Max did in the beginning was innocent enough, but I always had the fear he would escalate.

He didn't, though. Not in high school.

And now, it seems unclear. His expression isn't mean or cold, it's warm. Like the more he looks at me, the more he implores me to understand, the happier he gets.

I'm going to be sick.

I clear my throat. "I don't think we're on the same page about that."

He approaches. I back up, hitting the seat of Royal's cubby. My knees almost fold, but I manage to stay on my feet.

He grasps at me. My forearms. His hands slide down to my wrists, then my hands. His gaze bores into my face. "Harper. I left you flowers. I was telling you that you're it for me, baby. You're *it* for me. When you disappeared, I was devastated. But then fate put us back on the same path, and suddenly I could see again."

Disappeared? It's called going to college and not informing your stalker.

But I followed Royal, and my brother is easy to track. There are articles online about him, his performance, his stats. He plays for a great college—he's going to the NHL. They say he's one of the top prospects for this summer's draft. Whoever *they* are.

If Max Keegan wanted to find me, all he had to do was find Royal.

And sure enough… that's what he did. But by the sounds of it, he didn't expect it to be so easy.

"I have a plan this time," he continues. "I've got a job all lined up in San Francisco. You'll never have to work a day in your life. And the weather there—it's gorgeous. My family used to vacation there. You're going to love it."

"I want to work."

It just comes out—but it's true. Max and I have never seen eye to eye. *Clearly.* But what does he want me to do? Sit at home? Wait for him to return? Keep the house clean, cook dinner, service *him*, and rely on his income?

Never.

His next step forward, into my space, is more deliberate. I try to step back, but my heels bump into the seat in front of Royal's cubby again. His grip tightens subtly on my hands, keeping me from sidestepping away.

"You know, it's kind of cute how your roommate thought I was your brother."

My blood runs cold. I didn't think of that—I mean, I should've. It was right there in front of my face. I even *thought* it… but Cynthia said he was an FSU hockey player. Clearly, seeing him dressed now, he's been playing the part.

"Let me prove my devotion to you, baby." He brushes his knuckles down my jaw. "Or I'll break your brother's leg and make sure he never plays hockey again. But that's your choice, okay?"

A chill runs down my spine.

He smiles and touches me again. My cheek. Just to prove he can.

And I let him. I stay where I am, frozen in place for a solid few seconds, until my senses return. I jerk away, staggering to the side. I yank my hand from his and put space between us, but this room, this whole arena, suddenly seems too small to contain both of us.

I'm too claustrophobic with Max nearby.

His gaze slips toward predatory. "Maybe whatever injury Royal sustains could affect Camden Church, too. He's the one in your videos, isn't he?"

Oh, fuck. The WatchMe account?

Camden never showed his face, though, so how—

"You think I would let you stay in that house, full of untrustworthy hockey players, and not look out for you?"

He yanks my arm. I stumble after him, trying to keep my footing with his quick pace. My mind whirls, but no immediate solution presents itself. No way to get out of this without him escaping to come back another day and hurt Royal.

Or Camden.

"He snuck into your room. He defiled you while you slept, and you fucking woke up with your hand down your panties." His voice is hard. "You think that's forgivable?"

My eyes burn, but he doesn't seem to notice. I don't know how to handle this.

"I packed you a bag." He gestures. "So you don't have to see those awful men again. Your brother"—his voice cracks—"he let his friend assault you time and again, and he did *nothing*. Did he even notice? Did he not lay awake wondering if his baby sister was safe in his house?"

"I was safe there," I say in a low voice.

"No, you were NOT!"

I flinch back like he struck me. He scowls and turns away, and I sink into the seat at my back. I lean against one of the side walls of the cubby and risk a glance upward.

C. Church.

Fitting.

When he turns back around, he has a pink rose in his hand. He comes forward and kneels in front of me, offering it out.

"Like it?" he asks, breathless.

No. No, no, I hate it.

My stomach rolls, and I swallow a few times to try and beat back the nausea. When I don't move to accept it, he forcibly takes my hand and curls my fingers around the thornless stem.

I squeeze my eyes shut. He was the threat that never seemed *threatening*. Besides the roses he left in my room... that was creepy as fuck. But now, he's escalated just like I've always feared. Everything I've read about how to deal with a stalker, how to placate them, has gone out the window.

All I can think is, I will not let him remove me from this place against my will.

If he's escalating, it means *I* need to escalate.

I open my eyes and focus on the rose in my hand. My fingers tremble when I reach up and pinch one of the petals. I have a bruise on my thigh from where Camden pinched me last night. Crushing the velvet pink between my fingers reminds me of skin.

The floral scent assaults me, and I exhale a long, slow breath.

"There," he murmurs. "You're coming to your senses, aren't you, baby?"

I stay silent.

"Now, there's just one question that remains." He pauses. His hands come to my knees, hot even through my jeans. "Was Camden Church the one in the videos?"

My breath catches. "What?"

"The WatchMe account, Harper." His gaze darkens. "I saw what he did to you, and it matches some videos. But beyond that, I had to watch you demean yourself on your knees in front of him. Did you do that to test me? To send the message that I wasn't doing enough?"

I rear back. "What? No."

"Baby, I'm going to need you to delete those videos."

"I—" I can't exactly say I don't have access to them.

That probably wouldn't go over so well.

I set the flower aside and lean even farther back. He rises up on his knees, and he's so much bigger than me that our faces are even like this.

I can't do this.

"He's never going to play hockey again," Max decides. "I know I said that about Royal, but I mean it, Harper. You're mine. You've been mine. And suddenly he thinks he can come in here and lay claim? Absolutely not."

A chill sweeps down my spine.

"Give me your phone." He drums his fingers on my knees.

I shake my head, but when his expression flickers to ice-cold, I find myself complying. He unlocks it without hesitation, typing in my code, and taps around on the screen. A second later, he tosses it aside.

Out of reach.

"He'll come here. You'll sit like a good little girl while I make sure he never hurts you again." He rubs my thighs.

My eyes widen. "You can't—"

He sighs. "Is it because you liked what he did to you?"

It's not like that.

"I can do that, if you really need it." He leans in and catches the back of my head. He drags his mouth from my jaw up to my ear. "I can fuck you like a dirty whore and leave you tied up to the radiator like a free-use bitch, to be ready and waiting for me whenever I want. If that's what you need."

Revulsion slides through me.

My hand moves behind me, groping for something—*anything*—to help me.

I brush the toe of Camden's skate and go still. Max doesn't notice. His grip on the back of my head relaxes the slightest bit, and he drops his mouth to my neck. He kisses me there, hot and sloppy, his tongue tasting my skin.

I am not in my body.

It's like I separate myself from it, not feeling it. Not reacting. I let him touch me and I hate myself for it. But I grip the skate and slide my finger along the blade behind my back.

My gaze lands on the rose.

He ruined roses for me. He ruined *surprises* for me. And being able to post my location in real time. Every social media post is delayed, any hints about where I truly am has been cloaked for the last few months. All in an effort to hide from Max.

With my free hand, I touch his arm.

He hums, content. Then groans when my hand moves to the back of his neck.

Then his hair. I knock the hat off to get a better grip, the strands just long enough to thread my fingers through.

I picture Max breaking Camden's leg—or worse. The snap of bone is audible in my ears, an unwelcome echo that guides my movements.

The out-of-body experience only worsens when I tighten my hold and yank his head back. His eyes are glazed, his lips wet, mouth parted.

I move fast, the skate heavy in my hand, but I can't think. Can't process what I'm about to do. I drive it forward, across his neck. The blade catches on his skin, and it's not smooth enough to be easy.

It *rips*.

The spurt of blood is shockingly violent. It hits my face and chest, splattering across my neck. *Pause.* Then again. His eyes widen in horror, mirroring mine.

I just did that.

I shove him away, and he goes, stumbling, trying to figure out what happened. He cups his neck, trying to stop the flow of blood. But it rushes through his fingers, dripping to the floor between us, while he gapes and gurgles.

He can't save himself, can he?

"I will not live in fear of you," I whisper.

His expression morphs into anger, and he suddenly stumbles back toward me. He releases his throat and grasps at me. His blood makes his hold slick, unstable, but he's strong enough that it doesn't matter. He pulls me with him, down on top of him, and fear floods through me that he's going to use his last breath to kill me, too. His hands go around my throat, even as the blood gushes from his.

I scream and thrash, my lungs burning. I just need to last longer than him. And finally, his grip goes slack. I fall away from him and skitter backward, dragging my knees up to my chest. I wheeze, inhaling as deep as I can.

It doesn't seem like enough. My head swims.

Suddenly, someone moves in front of me. My view of Max is blocked. Hands grab my shoulders and shake me, and I flinch. I keep going, trying to evade, but the hands are too strong.

"Stop. It's me."

Camden.

My gaze finally lifts and locks on to his face.

Oh, God. My eyes fill with tears, but he shakes me. *Hard.*

"No," he snaps. "Don't go into shock. Don't freak out on me, little Lawson." He glances over his shoulder, then meets my gaze. "What're the odds this is the stalker you talked about before?"

My throat works, and it takes a long moment for a rasping answer to come out. "Hundred percent."

He seems to consider.

"Okay," he finally says. "Get in the shower."

"W-what?"

"Shower. Through that door over there. You're covered in blood."

When I don't move, he propels me out of the locker room and into the showers. Unlike all the girls' locker rooms I've seen in the past, this one just has open stalls without curtains. He guides me into one, clothes and all, and turns on the water.

A minute later, there's a bar of soap in my hand.

When I don't move, he grimaces and goes for my shirt. I raise my arms for him to remove it, my resistance gone. He has me brace a hand on his shoulder while he kneels down and helps me out of my pants.

In my underwear, I step under the now-hot stream. It brings some of my mind back, and I rotate to find Camden still standing in front of me.

There's a bloody handprint on his shirt. On the shoulder where I gripped him.

My stomach rolls.

"Is he dead?" I lick my lips.

The metallic taste of blood fills my mouth, and I gag.

I rotate around and brace my hand on the wall, my stomach cramping. The vomit sears my throat. I get a glimpse of the blood staining my hands.

"Don't lose it on me. We'll get it off."

He steps closer, avoiding the stream of water, and plucks the soap from my hands. He lathers it in his hands and scrubs at mine, dunking them under the water until I can see my pale skin again.

"You've got it from here." He clears his throat and steps back. "Scrub everything. I'll be back."

It's all I can do to follow instructions. I face the water again, rinsing my face. Cleaning the blood from my neck, my chest. When I finally feel like I'm clean enough, and the water swirling around my feet is no longer tinted pink, I shut off the tap and step out.

There's a towel waiting for me, along with familiar clothes.

My clothes.

My hairbrush and deodorant.

What the fuck?

It dawns on me that it all came from the bag Max brought in.

He really was planning on whisking me away.

I never would've returned to Framingham.

The thought makes me cold inside. I hurry to dry and dress, combing out my hair in hurried strokes.

When I exit back into the main locker room, Max is covered in a tarp and Camden sits in front of his cubby, his skate in his hand. There's blood on the blade.

This time, licking my lips doesn't give me the taste of blood. His expression is blank. Careful. He seems to be considering something, and that consideration doesn't involve looking at me.

"You've always been a liability," he eventually says. "To me. To my career. To your brother."

I freeze. "W-what?"

"When did you know he was in Framingham, Harper?"

My mouth dries, and I shake my head. I don't have an answer, and it's then I notice he has the rose in his other hand. He sets down the skate, ignoring the blood, and runs the tip of his index finger along the edge of one of the petals.

"You saw him at a game, and it was then you mentioned the pink flowers he used to leave. I had forgotten that detail." He scoffs. "I was confused why there were over a dozen roses in the bin. Confused by your non-reaction to it. But now, I think I understand."

He sets it aside and focuses on me.

"Did you think it was me?"

Guilt heats my cheeks, and I nod. I can't deny it. I didn't know who to suspect—him or Max. But it remains true that I couldn't tell Royal.

"I'm going to handle this for you." He points to the tarp. To the *body* under it. "I'll make it go away. If I don't, you're either going to drag all of us through a trial where they smear *you* to bits trying to make Max Keegan look innocent, or you're just going to plead out and go straight to fucking jail."

"It's self-defense," I whisper.

"They won't care. That's the way this world works,

Harper. No one wants to see a woman protect herself. You'd be punished for it."

My eyes burn, and my vision blurs. He's right about that much. How many rapists get probation, or nothing at all? How many victims are retraumatized on the stand while trying to get justice?

Too many.

And what kind of questions would they ask about Max's death?

Did you report his stalking to the authorities? Yes... in high school.

But not recently? No, I kept that a secret.

So you have no proof besides your word? You disposed of evidence? Right...

And did you ever rebuff Max's attempts? Not in so many words.

Straight to prison. I'm not made for prison. I think I'm a relatively strong-willed person, but I don't know if I could handle incarceration.

"I'll handle it," Camden reiterates.

This feels a bit like making a deal with the devil. I skirt around the tarp and drop my hair brush into the open bag sitting beside him. Along with my favorite clothes and toiletries, Max somehow thought to pack my makeup, wallet, and the rented camera from my photography class. The corner of my silver laptop, and a bit of the charging cable, is visible under the clothes.

Strange.

"What do you want in return for this?"

His eyes positively burn. "You cannot ruin Royal's future, Harper. Which means: you disappear."

"Disappear?"

"I don't care if you talk to your parents. But you do not go home. You don't talk to your brother. You stay far, far away from us."

Us. He's including himself in that, then?

His first threat... his first promise, as it was, floats back to the forefront of my mind. *I can give you mercy, or I'll drag you into ruin. Your choice.*

In the end, I suppose, this sort of ruin *is* on me. I suffered his mercy for weeks.

Can I really pick up and vanish? Start a new life somewhere else? My parents will be confused, but I think it might crush Royal. At first, at least. If Camden came up with some plausible excuse, some horrible lie to tell my brother, it might make my absence easier to swallow.

Now, I'm choosing to ruin myself instead of my brother.

In the end, it's not Camden's doing at all. It's mine.

And *fuck*, why does this hurt so bad? I may as well have cracked open my chest and pulled out my lungs.

"I'll go."

He nods, accepting my answer. "I know."

"My parents—"

"I don't care what lie you have to tell them," he interrupts. "If I hear that you've spoken to Royal, all this comes back to bite you. I'll frame it however I want. That Max was our friend and you always had a crush on him. That you were the obsessed one. That Royal warned you to leave him alone..."

"I already said I'd go," I snip. "No need to twist the knife."

His lips curl. "You did plenty with my skate. I don't have to twist anything."

I hate him.

He points to my phone, sitting plugged into an outlet on the far wall. "I outfitted your phone with some new apps, as well as a train ticket to get you started."

I unplug my phone and roll up the charger, stuffing it back in the bag. I zip it shut and hoist it over my shoulder.

I check my phone screen, only to see that he's already called me a car from the rideshare app. It's three minutes away.

"How?" I ask.

And I hope he knows I'm asking *how the hell* he's going to handle this. Because he's only a year older than me, and I don't have a freaking clue.

"That's for me to know." He jerks his chin toward the exit. "And you to hopefully never find out."

I take one last look at him. His perfect fucking face. The chill in his expression.

He doesn't care at all. He doesn't seem to even mind about the body lying several feet away from him, and the blood sprayed across the locker room.

"Go," he orders.

I hate him. I repeat that when I pause to pull on my shoes. I repeat it when I exit the locker room, my spine straight, not daring to look back. I say it again out on the sidewalk.

When I'm in the car.

When my ticket is scanned on the train to Boston.

I hate him, I tell myself when I shed the first of many, *many* tears.

My heart breaks, and no one on the train gives a shit about my crying. About my life being ripped out from under me.

About never seeing my brother again.

When I unlock my phone screen and go through the new apps. Then, reflexively, I check WatchMe, only to find my stalking account has been logged out—and *The Voyeur* account has been logged in.

I can finally see the exact number of paying subscribers, and the bank account that's connected is now also on my phone. It's in my name.

He gave me control of this one thing while ripping away all the rest.

So why does it feel like the thinnest of lifelines?

I take a breath and fight the instinct to delete the whole page. I can't—not if I am going to survive on my own. No asking my brother for help. I can't handle asking my parents either. Telling them anything but the truth will fall short, and I will not risk that.

Camden said to make something up, but I don't have a single thought in my head. No lie to justify why I'm running away.

I block Royal's number and shut down my phone. I rest my head against the train window. My breath comes out in a long, slow exhale.

I'm on my own. It's terrifying. It's disorienting.

But it also feels like freedom.

TO BE CONTINUED in *Ruined God*.

Grab a special bonus scene (from Camden's POV) here: https://dl.bookfunnel.com/jz2zaq7qeu

WHERE TO FIND SARA

Thank you so much for coming along on this crazy journey with me.

If you like my stories, I'd highly encourage you to come join my Facebook group, S. Massery Squad. There's a lot of fun stuff happening in there, and they're who I go to for polls about future books, where I share teasers, etc!

My Patreon is also an awesome place to connect and get exclusive content! On release months, I do signed paperbacks. Plus, get ARCs, audiobooks, and artwork before the rest of the world. Find me here: http://patreon.com/smassery

And last but not least, here are some social media links for ya:

Facebook: Author S Massery

Instagram: @authorsmassery
Tiktok: @smassery
Goodreads: S. Massery
Bookbub: S. Massery

ABOUT THE AUTHOR

S. Massery is a dark romance author who loves injecting a good dose of suspense into her stories. Originally from Massachusetts, she now lives in Southern California with her dog, Alice.

Before adventuring into the world of writing, she went to college in Boston and held a wide variety of jobs—including working on a dude ranch in Wyoming (a personal highlight). She has a love affair with coffee and chocolate. When S. Massery isn't writing, she can be found devouring books, playing outside with her dog, or trying to make people smile.

Join her newsletter to stay up to date on new releases: http://smassery.com/newsletter

#3 Stolen Crown

Broken Mercenaries

#1 Blood Sky

#2 Angel of Death

#3 Morning Star

More at http://smassery.com

9 781957 286303